"Have You Met The Local Law?"

the restaurant owner asked Sarah.

She frowned. "The local law?"

"This here is Jake Wolfe. He's one of the Sprucewood police. Jake, this is Sarah Cummings."

Jake turned to Sarah with a smile—one of his most charming. "Miss Cummings," he murmured, extending his right hand.

Sarah Cummings didn't appear charmed at all; she looked wary, almost frightened. But she did give him her hand. "Officer Wolfe," she said, so softly he could barely hear her. She didn't return his smile and drew back her hand after the briefest contact with his palm.

Hmm... Sarah was looking at him as if he were the devil incarnate. And she appeared on the point of making a dash for the door. Very intriguing...

Dear Reader,

It's hard for me to believe that summer is almost over and autumn is right around the corner. For those of us who live where it gets cold, that means we have to start pulling out our sweaters and bundling up our bodies. (If you live where it's warm all year-round, well, we'll just envy you the good weather!) And if you have kids, it's time for them to go off to school, probably providing you with some wonderful quiet time!

During that quiet time I hope you'll pick up more than one of this month's terrific Silhouette Desire romances. We have some special treats in store for you! First, there's the start of a new miniseries from Ann Major called SOMETHING WILD. Its first book, *Wild Honey* is the *Man of the Month.* Next, we have *another* wonderful series, BIG BAD WOLFE, from the talented pen of Joan Hohl. The first book here is *Wolfe Waiting.*

The month is completed with four more romantic, sensuous, compelling love stories. Raye Morgan brings us her unique brand of magic in *Caution: Charm at Work;* Carole Buck heats up the pages with *Sparks;* Anne Marie Winston creates something very wonderful and unusual in *Chance at a Lifetime;* and Caroline Cross makes a sparkling debut with *Dangerous.*

So take time off *for yourself*—you deserve the break—and curl up with a Silhouette Desire!

All the Best,

Lucia Macro
Senior Editor

JOAN HOHL
WOLFE WAITING

SILHOUETTE *Desire*
™ Published by Silhouette Books New York
America's Publisher of Contemporary Romance

SILHOUETTE BOOKS
300 East 42nd St., New York, N.Y. 10017

WOLFE WAITING

Copyright © 1993 by Joan Hohl

ISBN: 0-373-05806-3

First Silhouette Books printing September 1993

All the characters in this book have no existence outside the imagination of the author and have no relation whatsoever to anyone bearing the same name or names. They are not even distantly inspired by any individual known or unknown to the author, and all incidents are pure invention.

® and ™: Trademarks used with authorization. Trademarks indicated with ® are registered in the United States Patent and Trademark Office, the Canada Trade Mark Office and in other countries.

Printed in the U.S.A.

Books by Joan Hohl

Silhouette Desire

A Much Needed Holiday #247
*Texas Gold #294
*California Copper #312
*Nevada Silver #330
Lady Ice #354
One Tough Hombre #372
Falcon's Flight #390
The Gentleman Insists #475
Christmas Stranger #540
Handsome Devil #612
Convenient Husband #732
Lyon's Cub #762
†*Wolfe Waiting* #806

Silhouette Intimate Moments

Moments Harsh, Moments Gentle #35

Silhouette Special Edition

Thorne's Way #54
Forever Spring #444
Thorne's Wife #537

Silhouette Romance

A Taste for Rich Things #334
Someone Waiting #358
The Scent of Lilacs #376

Silhouette Books

Silhouette Summer Sizzlers 1988
"Grand Illusion"

*Desire trilogy
†Big, Bad Wolfe Series

JOAN HOHL,

a Gemini and inveterate daydreamer, says she always has her head in the clouds. An avid reader all her life, she discovered romances about ten years ago. "And as soon as I read one," she confesses, "I was hooked." Now an extremely prolific author, she is thrilled to be getting paid for doing exactly what she loves best.

One

She might have looked beautiful, if not for the big, round tortoiseshell glasses that gave her a wide-eyed owlish appearance.

Jake Wolfe sat at the counter of the off-campus hamburger joint, nursing a cup of coffee while surreptitiously appraising the young woman seated in the corner booth.

She had a good face, great bone structure, a mass of gorgeous dark brown hair tumbling in vibrant waves to somewhere below her shoulders. Her slim, elegant nose was pointed at the book lying open on the table in front of her.

"Refill?" Dave, the counterman, asked, coming to a halt opposite Jake, coffee pot poised over his cup.

"Umm..." Jake murmured, reluctantly shifting his attention to the man. "Who's the owl perched in the corner?"

"Name's Cummings," Dave said, not looking away from the dark stream pouring from the pot. "Sarah. She's nice."

A man of a few words was Dave, Jake mused, nodding his thanks for the refill. Getting information out of Dave was not unlike mining for hens' molars.

"New to the college?" Jake pried at Dave's closed lips. "A graduate student?"

"Nah." Dave shook his head. "Well, yeah, she is new to the college, but she's not a student. She's the new associate professor of the historical studies department."

"History teacher, huh?" Jake grimaced. "I was always bored in history class." A devilish grin played with his mouth. "Now, if I had had a teacher that looked like that..." He let his voice fade and shot a meaningful glance at the woman.

"I hear you." Dave chuckled. "Seemed like every one of my teachers was old, wore rusty-looking black dresses and serviceable black shoes with thick heels and laces. And every blessed one of them carried a ruler—used it, too."

A veritable mouthful for the taciturn Dave. Jake flashed him a sparkling white-toothed grin. A blur of movement caught his eye, and he cast a sidelong look at the corner booth. The owl had closed her book and was sliding off the bench seat.

"Er . . . Dave," he murmured. "Why don't you introduce me to the lady professor?"

"Dunno." Dave leveled a pointed look at Jake's uniform. "Ain't you on duty?"

"So what?" Jake retorted in a whisper. The owl was now standing, gathering her things together, taking off the glasses and confirming his speculation—she *was* beautiful. "Get with the program," he muttered. "I'll meet her sooner or later. I patrol the campus, remember? It might as well be sooner."

She was walking toward him. Jake held his breath and glared a warning at Dave. Dave got the message—and the implied threat.

"Oh, Miss Cummings." Dave stopped her at the stool next to Jake's. "Have you met the local law?"

She started and frowned. "The local law?"

Jake had to quash an urge to raise his hand and smooth the frown line from her brow with his fingertips. He released his breath in an exasperated sigh; why was he plagued by folks like Dave, forever honing their meager comedic talents on him?

Dave obviously heard the sigh, because he immediately pulled his act together. "Uh, yeah, this here's Jake Wolfe. He's one of the Sprucewood police. Patrols the campus." He laid a benign smile on Jake. "Jake, this is Miss Cummings."

Jake shrugged off Dave's smile and turned to Sarah with one of his own, his most charming. "Miss Cummings," he murmured, extending his right hand.

Sarah Cunnings didn't appear at all charmed; she looked wary, almost frightened. But she did give him her hand. "Officer Wolfe," she said, so softly he could barely hear her. She didn't return his smile, and she drew her hand back after the briefest contact with his palm.

Hmm... Now Jake frowned. Sarah Cummings was looking at him as if he were the devil incarnate. And she appeared on the point of making a dash for the door. What was this woman's problem? he wondered.

"Dave tells me you're the new associate professor of the history department," he said, sliding off the stool to stand directly in her path.

"Ah, yes, I...ah, am."

What in hell? Now Jake was really confused. Unless he was misreading her tone, Sarah was as nervous as a rookie cop on his first big case.

"You know, it's funny we haven't run across each other before," Jake observed in a neutral tone, careful not to betray his aroused suspicion. "Did you arrive just recently?"

"Yes." She nodded, and sent a quick glance at the door. "I, er... arrived two weeks ago."

"Yeah, that's right," Dave confirmed. "I remember you came in for lunch the day after you got here."

"That explains it, then. I was working the middle and late shifts the last two weeks," Jake drawled, favoring Dave with a get-lost look.

"Yeah, that's right," Dave repeated, all in a rush. "And I gotta get back to work." Grabbing a cloth, he began wiping his way down the counter.

Jake waited; nothing happened. Sarah Cummings just stood there, fidgeting and looking as if she'd prefer to be anywhere else but there.

"Are you from this area?" Jake asked, digging for a common denominator.

"No." Sarah Cummings shook her head. "I'm from Maryland..." She hesitated, as if she didn't want to give him any more information than was absolutely necessary. "Baltimore," she added, when he didn't respond—or move.

"Nice city," Jake said, trying another smile; it fell flat. "I've been to the Harbor Place."

"Oh, have you?" She didn't smile; she eyed the door. "Um, I, er... That's nice."

Great. Jake wasn't at all sure he could handle such scintillating conversation. What he felt certain of was her intense desire to get away from him. Why? Since he couldn't convince himself that she was overwhelmed by his masculine attractions, he was at a loss to explain her strange reaction to meeting him. Maybe she was shy? Retiring? In trouble? Jake dismissed the last consideration as springing from his occupational mind-set. Miss Owl Eyes looked too young and innocent to have the kind of trouble that would make her wary of a police officer.

Had his deodorant failed him? Mentally shaking off the flip reflection, Jake tried another gambit. "Can I buy you a cup of coffee?'' he asked, flicking a hand at the stool next to her. "That is, if you're not in a hurry?''

"No...thank you..." She didn't even hesitate in refusing, and he wasn't surprised. "I, ah...have a class. Another time, perhaps." Sarah Cummings swept a telling look over the full six-foot-four-inch length of his obstructive body. "May I pass, please?''

What could he say? Or do? Swallowing a curse, Jake said and did the only permissible thing. "Of course," he murmured, dredging up a smile as he stepped aside. Inspiration struck as she started to move by him. "When?''

"When?" She paused to glance at him in consternation. "When what?''

"You said another time," he answered, shooting a quick look at his wrist watch. "I stop in here for my morning coffee break every day about this time," he explained, moving his shoulders in a shrug. "How 'bout tomorrow?''

"Oh...well, I..." Her eyes shifted from him to the door then back to him. "I..."

"The invitation's only for coffee," Jake inserted, in a reasonable tone aimed at reassurance.

Sarah Cummings wet her lips. The nervous action sent an astounding shaft of heat sizzling through Jake's body, forcing him to breathe slowly while waiting for her response.

"All right," she finally said, with unconcealed reluctance. "Ten o'clock?''

"Fine." Jake smiled. "I'll be here."

Then she was gone. But she didn't scurry away, as Jake had expected her to. No. Sarah Cummings walked in a supple, long-legged stride, neatly rounded hips swaying just a fraction from side to side.

A goddess. She walks like a goddess. Jake rubbed his suddenly damp palms against his taut thighs and blinked himself out of bemusement, back into reality.

Whoa! You'd better be careful here, Wolfe, he advised himself. This woman is potent.

"Oh...those eyes!" Jake said, grinning at Dave as he slid back onto the stool.

"Yeah, they're brown," Dave retorted, obviously unimpressed by the subject of eye color.

"Brown? Brown?" Jake demanded. "Are you blind, man? Sarah Cummings eyes are not merely brown." He pondered a moment before continuing. "Her eyes have the look of spring pansies...that soft, velvety brown."

Dave grimaced. "Oh, brother."

"You have no soul, Dave," Jake said accusingly, keeping a straight face. "No appreciation for nuances."

"Maybe so," Dave allowed. "But I recognize a nice person when I meet one, and Miss Cummings is the genuine article."

"Hmm..." Jake concurred with a definite nod of his head. But what is she afraid of? And why does she appear fearful of me? Because of the uniform—and what it represents?

His interest piqued on several levels, Jake sipped his now-tepid coffee and kept his own counsel.

Drat the man.

Gnawing on her lower lip, Sarah strode along the campus walkway, heading for the humanities building. Distracted, she responded absently to the greetings called out to her by several students making their way to the class she would be conducting within the next fifteen minutes.

Why had she agreed to have coffee with him? Sarah asked herself, smiling her thanks to the pretty young woman holding the door open for her into the lecture hall.

Because he was so darned intimidating, she admitted, moving to the front of the large room. An image rose to fill her mind, an overwhelming image that caused a tremor in her hands as she deposited her handbag and books on the table.

Even the image was intimidating. A frown creased her brow as she slid her glasses into place and set her stopwatch and her text on the lectern. She had not discerned an inch of excess flesh on his body, and with his tall frame and whipcord-lean form, Jake Wolfe was one formidable specimen of masculinity.

Handsome, too... in a rugged, chiseled way.

"Good morning, class. Shall we begin?"

Hair the shade of golden toast.

"Though the Western world was barely aware of it, the Chinese Empire was already great when the Romans began their quest to conquer the Mediterranean."

Eyes the dark blue color of a twilight sky.

"That is an excellent point, Mr. Kluesewitz. China did not fall far short of the power and wealth that the Roman Empire achieved, even at its zenith."

Skin tone a deep, tanned bronze.

"Yes, of course, I do agree that China left for posterity a wonderful legacy of literary and visual artworks."

So tall, so imposing, every solid inch of him an assault on feminine senses.

A police officer.

"...also known as the Period of the Warring States, nearly two hundred years of turmoil following the collapse of the Zhou dynasty."

Purely by rote, Sarah somehow managed to conduct the class on the ancient Chinese Empire. The shuffling of feet directed her gaze to the watch; the period was over. Wondering if anything she had said made any sense, she thanked the students for their participation and dismissed the class.

A police officer.

Sarah sighed as she collected her things.

And she had foolishly agreed to meet him tomorrow morning for coffee.

Was she looking for more trouble . . . or for help?

Sarah worried the question throughout her remaining classes for the day and during the brisk fifteen-minute walk from the campus to the apartment she had rented on the second floor of a recently converted private home in the small town of Sprucewood. Since she enjoyed the walk, Sarah seldom took her car out of the tenants' garage in back of the house.

Not even the brilliance of the southeastern Pennsylvania autumn, the nip in the air or the tangy scent of burning leaves had the power to divert her attention from the mishmash of her own thoughts.

Sarah had a definite problem.

Could Officer Jake Wolfe be the solution?

No. No. Sarah denied the ray of hope. She couldn't confide in Jake Wolfe, or any other person connected with the law. Talking, speculating, was too dangerous. There were lives involved here, the lives of others—and possibly even her own.

Silence is golden, Miss Cummings.

The warning echo of the student's voice whispered through Sarah's mind, bringing a shiver to her flesh that was unrelated to the zip in the early-October air.

No—talking, especially to Jake Wolfe, was definitely not one of her options. In truth, she felt she had no options, no recourse at all in the matter.

Beginning to feel mentally and emotionally battered, Sarah entered her apartment, dropped her things onto a chair, kicked off her shoes and padded through the living room and into the tiny, utilitarian kitchen.

She had felt too tense to eat anything at lunch time, but even worry eventually gave way to encroaching hunger. With a sensation growing inside her of her stomach having taken on the dimensions of a huge hole in the earth, Sarah began gathering together the ingredients for a macaroni-cheese-and-broccoli casserole.

After placing the baking dish in the oven, Sarah set the timer, slid a bottle of white wine into the fridge to chill and headed for the bathroom for a long, scented and—she hoped—relaxing soak in the tub.

The oven timer was ringing when Sarah emerged, pink and glowing, from the bathtub. And so was the doorbell.

Now who in the world could that be? Grumbling to herself about visitors showing up unexpectedly at dinnertime, Sarah grabbed the garment hanging from the hook on the inside of the bathroom door.

Pulling the lilac-striped satin robe over her nude, still-damp body, she drew the braided belt into a tight slipknot as she crossed the living room.

The bell trilled again as she neared the front door.

"Yes, who is it?" she called, reaching confidently for the doorknob.

"Jake Wolfe." His voice was muffled but unmistakable through the wooden panel.

Her hand paused to hang in midair an inch from the knob. Her heart seemed to stop beating for an instant, then accelerated to an alarming rate. Her throat went dry; her palms grew moist. Her mind went blank.

"Miss Cummings?"

Sarah swallowed, opened her mouth, then swallowed again before she could force one word from her parched lips.

"Yes?"

"Are you going to open the door?"

Was she? Sarah frowned and glanced down at the thin, shimmery material covering her nudity. No way.

"I'm not dressed," she said, raising her voice to penetrate the door.

"So go get dressed," he shot back. "I'll wait."

Checkmate. Undecided whether to do as he suggested or tell him to buzz off, Sarah raked a hand through the steam-dampened, tangled mass of her hair and curled her bare toes into the soft nap of the carpet.

The timer bell was jangling away merrily in the kitchen; she didn't hear it.

"Ah . . . Sarah, are you still there?"

She started. Had he heard her breathing? Ridiculous. Sarah shook off the idea.

"Yes, I'm here."

"Is that a smoke alarm I hear?"

His query jolted her into awareness. The casserole! Sarah shot a glance at the kitchen, then back at the door. Since it was obvious that he was not going to budge, there was no help for it—she would eventually have to open the door.

Besides, she was hungry.

"Do I smell something burning?"

Burning? Her beautiful casserole! Jake's question galvanized her into action. Twisting the lock, she turned the knob and swung the door open, and then, without actually looking at him, seeing him, spun to dash for the kitchen.

"Come in," she said over her shoulder as she rushed into the tiny room. "I'll be with you in a few minutes."

A tingling sensation crept up Sarah's spine as she bent over the open oven door to remove the baking dish. She hadn't heard a sound, yet she knew Jake Wolfe had followed her into the kitchen and was standing behind her... too close behind her.

"Can I help?"

Even knowing he was there, Sarah started at the easy and too attractive sound of his voice. "No! Ah..." She grimaced at the fluttery tremor in her voice. "Thank you, but no." Her back still to him, she placed the casserole on top of the stove, closed the oven door, then switched off the timer.

The sudden silence rattled her more than the jangling sound of the timer had.

Jake had moved into the room, even closer to her. Sarah heard his slow inhaling and exhaling.

"Not burned," he murmured. "Smells delicious." He hesitated a moment before continuing. "Cheese? Broccoli? Right?"

"Yes," Sarah replied, on a sharp sigh. She turned, and nearly jumped back against the stove; he was standing too damned close. "If you will excuse me?"

Her voice now held a decided edge. "I would like to get dressed."

Sarah wasn't quite sure what reaction she'd expected from him. Perhaps a slow examination of her scantily clad person, followed by an insinuating, cocky grin. If so, she was off the mark. Jake Wolfe kept his eyes fixed on hers, and not by the wildest stretch of the imagination could his smile be described as anything but pleasant and friendly.

"Sure." He backed up, through the doorway, into the living room. "I'll wait here."

"You do that," Sarah muttered, sweeping by him on a direct path to her bedroom.

"Anything I can do to help?"

His question brought her to a jarring halt in the open doorway to her room. Uh-huh. Here it comes, the offer to zip a zipper, snap a snap, hook a bra clasp. "Like . . . what?" she asked through gritted teeth.

"Set the table." He responded, neatly throwing her off balance. "I mean, you can't be so cruel as to expose a man to such tantalizing aromas and then not invite him to stay for dinner."

Sarah slowly turned to give him an arch look. "Can't I?" she inquired coolly. "Why can't I?"

Jake Wolfe managed a woeful expression. "It would be cruel and unusual punishment for a hungry man."

It was at that moment that Sarah saw him . . . really saw him. And what she saw did quite a number on her senses and her nervous system.

Jake was out of uniform, which should have produced a diminishing effect. It didn't. On the contrary, the change of attire had the effect of a sensual power charge.

Whoever would have thought of denim as an electrical conductor? Sarah marveled, staring at him while trying to appear casual and unaffected.

And the denim clung so faithfully to every curve and contour of his slim waist, narrow hips and long, muscular legs. Her gaze rose, collided with a broad expanse of chest and wide shoulders, delineated by a snug-fitting knit pullover shirt. Below the hem of the short sleeves, his lightly haired forearms tapered to raw-boned wrists and long-fingered hands that rested loosely on his hips, just beneath a plain leather belt.

The overall picture Jake Wolfe presented to her was one of solid, blatant masculinity. His stance appeared casual, but Sarah wasn't deceived. He was coiled and waiting, silently challenging her to refuse his request for a meal.

Sarah wanted to meet his challenge, wanted to deny and defy him, but she didn't. And she wasn't even certain why she didn't—wasn't certain, or didn't care to question it. Instead, she caved in to his request.

"The plates are in the cabinet above the sink," she said abruptly, turning away. "The flatware in the drawer below. The napkins are on the table. I'll only be a minute."

"Take your time." His voice was low, soft, beguiling. "I'm not going anywhere."

That's what worries me, Sarah told herself, shutting the door between them. If she had only met him sooner, as recently as one week ago...but no, it wouldn't have made a difference, wouldn't have changed the situation.

What to do?

Sarah stood inside the door, unable to move for a long moment, fighting against the insidious and exciting sensation of anticipation that was dancing along her nervous system. She felt strangely exhilarated and exhausted at one and the same time. Eagerness vied with reluctance. Trepidation warred with daring. Eagerness and daring won the tussle. Honesty led the way.

She was attracted to Jake Wolfe, Sarah conceded, strongly attracted to him. The admission set her in motion. Allowing that she was very likely making a mistake, a mistake she would probably regret, she nevertheless hurriedly dressed, dragged a taming brush through her tangled hair and applied a quick pat of foundation to her flushed cheeks, a flick of mascara to her lashes, and a dash of lipstick to her mouth. Then, her heart racing, she made herself walk slowly from the bedroom into the living room.

The sight that met her surprised gaze brought Sarah to a dead stop three steps into the room. She had only been gone fifteen minutes or so, and yet in that short span of time, Jake Wolfe had apparently been a very busy man.

Jake was standing, waiting for her, on one side of the small table Sarah had placed in front of a window in the corner of the living room next to the kitchen. The table was set for two, with her best lacy place mats, dishes and stemmed wineglasses. The steaming casserole held pride of place in the center of the table. The opened bottle of wine she had put in the fridge to chill sat to one side of the casserole, breathing, and a tossed salad in a wooden bowl was set on the other side.

Salad? Sarah shifted a glance from the bowl to Jake. How in the world had he accomplished all this in less than a half hour?

A low hunger growl from her stomach drew Sarah from her bemused reverie. In all honesty, it really didn't matter how he had managed to get everything together so quickly. What did matter was that he had. Still, she couldn't resist an impish urge to tease him, just a little.

"Everything looks lovely." She sauntered across the room to the table. "But... no bread?" she asked, in a gently taunting tone.

"But... of course," Jake replied, tossing the taunt back at her. "I found some wheat rolls in the bread keeper. The oven was still hot, so I stuck them in to warm."

The smile he tossed along with the taunt wiped all thoughts of bread, casserole and salad from her mind. Sarah did think of the wine, but only because her throat suddenly felt parched and achy. The man possessed a positively electrifying smile, electrifying and energizing. Sarah felt singed, and she felt an overwhelming need to move ... anywhere.

"Ah ... I'll get the rolls," she volunteered, veering away from the table and escaping into the kitchen.

"I'll pour the wine," Jake offered, in a voice that contained a suspicious hint of suppressed laughter.

As she removed the rolls from the oven and placed them in a small breadbasket, Sarah was dismayed by the tremor in her fingers and the trembling sensation in her midsection. The thought struck her that her unusual physical reaction to a man she had so recently met did not augur well for a relaxing and congenially shared dinner.

Sarah's fears were subsequently proved groundless. Although she began the meal in a state of heightened nervous tension, within minutes of seating herself opposite Jake Wolfe she found herself at ease, laughing at his dryly related anecdotes about the more amusing aspects of his work.

"The woman was beside herself, wanted me to take the dog into custody," he was saying midway through the meal.

"Custody!" Sarah exclaimed, laughing. "A dog?"

"Wild, huh?" Jake grinned. "And all because the mutt growled and scared her precious cat."

Jake was so friendly, so natural, Sarah found herself reciprocating without a second thought.

"I had a cat when I was in high school," she said, taking a sip of wine. "The darned feline was so independent...used to stand and stare at me as if to say 'Leave me alone, I'm simply too lazy to be bothered.'"

"Yeah, that's the way they look." Jake laughed, and served himself another helping of the casserole.

"Do you have to deal with many animals?" Sarah asked, absently breaking a roll. "I mean, must you cope on a daily basis, like mailmen?"

"No." Jake shook his head, then he grinned. "The only thing I cope with on a daily basis is Mr. Bennet's power cocktail."

"You lost me," Sarah confessed, buttering a piece of the roll before popping it into her mouth.

"Mr. Bennet lives outside of town, along my patrol route. He's eighty-some years old, and in fantastic shape. He's alone since his wife died last year, and he's kinda adopted me. He knows my routine and waits for me in front of his house every morning with a drink that he calls a power cocktail." He made a face; Sarah giggled. "The stuff tastes god-awful, but damned if I'm not beginning to feel better for it."

"Really? In what way?"

Jake shrugged. "My energy level's up, and I have more stamina, that kind of thing."

"Incredible," Sarah murmured.

"So is this." He indicated the macaroni dish with his fork. "You're a good cook. It's delicious."

Sarah felt inordinately pleased, and flustered, by his compliment. "Thank you, but it's only a casserole," she said. "I tend to stick to simple fare."

"Well, in a world that seems to grow increasingly more complex," Jake observed, "I think there's a lot to be said for simplicity."

Simplicity. That one word dispersed the euphoric haze clouding Sarah's thought processes. Apart from her cooking, there was nothing simple about her life anymore. It had suddenly become very complicated, complicated and frightening. And absolutely the last person she should be relaxing with was a member of the local police force.

What if she had relaxed her guard to the point of inadvertently letting something slip? Sarah silently upbraided herself, concealing a shudder by turning away to glance at the kitchen wall clock.

"Oh, will you look at the time!" she exclaimed, in a not-altogether-exaggerated tone of shock. "I hate to ask you to eat and run, but..."

"You have a date?" Jake inserted, in a not-altogether-pleased tone of voice.

"That's really none of your business," she retorted. "But, no, I do not have a date. I have classroom work to prepare for tomorrow."

"Oh." Jake didn't appear chastened in the least. "Okay, but I'll help you clean up before I go."

"That's not necessary," Sarah insisted, moving away from the table in anticipation of his following her. "It'll only take a minute to clear the dishes and stack the dishwasher."

He hesitated, frowning at her.

Sarah held her breath.

He exhaled audibly, but gave in.

Sarah resumed breathing, and led the way to the door.

"I really am getting the bum's rush," he said, giving her a wry smile as he came to a stop next to her.

Sarah opened her mouth to apologize, then immediately closed it again and opened the door instead. Telling herself that she had nothing to apologize for, since he had invited himself to dinner, she offered him a sweet smile, along with a word of advice to send him on his way.

"Don't go away mad."

"Just go away," he finished the old saying for her in a droll tone. "Right?"

"I'm afraid so," she admitted, laughing out loud at his dejected expression.

"But you are still going to meet me for coffee tomorrow morning, aren't you?"

Sarah had forgotten about that. Knowing she shouldn't get within a mile of him again, she made a firm decision to say no.

"Yes." So much for firm decisions.

"Good." Raising his hand, Jake gave her a slight wave. "I'll see you, then. Thanks for dinner."

Sarah watched him lope down the stairs before shutting the door and slumping against it. Suddenly feeling drained, she sighed and closed her eyes.

Within the space of a few hours, her problems had doubled. Because Jake was as nice as he was handsome, she had enjoyed their interlude more than she could recall having enjoyed anything in a long time. She felt a strong attraction to him, an attraction that could be dangerous to her well-being.

Silence is golden.

Wincing at the echo in her memory, Sarah pushed away from the door and slowly crossed the room to the cluttered table. Staring down at the plate he had used, she experienced a sharp pang of regret for what might have been, had they met at any other time.

It wasn't fair, Sarah complained in silent despair.

Why did Jake Wolfe have to be so nice?

Two

Jake swallowed the last of the power cocktail, somehow managing not to gag or even grimace, and handed the tall glass through the open car window to the elderly man in the sweat suit who was standing by the side of the road.

"Thanks, Mr. Bennet." Jake made a show of glancing at the big circular watch on his wrist. "I gotta get moving. See you tomorrow morning."

"You betcha," the old gentleman called over the revving engine of the black-and-white. "And don't you go slacking off on your workouts."

"No, sir," Jake promised, checking the mirror before easing the car onto the macadam road.

Jake felt great. It was a spectacular autumn morning, the sunlight bright and warm, the air crisp and fresh. But Jake knew his feelings of well-being were not due entirely to the beneficial effects of the morning cocktail, or even the revitalizing results of the exercise program Mr. Bennet had suggested he try.

Jake was struck by the sudden, and mildly surprising, realization that his feelings of uncertainty and ambivalence about settling into a position as a small-town cop were easing somewhat—not altogether, as yet, but somewhat. It was a start on the road back to tradition for him. But even that startling realization wasn't the ultimate cause of his high spirits.

No, Jake was fully aware that the main ingredient supporting his inner sense of soundness and satisfaction stemmed directly from a human source.

Sarah Cummings.

Merely thinking her name brought a soft smile to tug at the corners of Jake's mouth.

Lord, what a woman.

With his outer eyes alertly skimming the area of his patrol route, Jake's inner eyes gazed at a memory image of Sarah, and the way she had appeared to him when she opened the apartment door the evening before.

Surrounded by a mass of steam-misted, gleaming dark hair, Sarah's lovely face had worn a becoming pink tinge from her recent bath. Her soft brown eyes had been shimmery, her lips moist, invitingly delicious-looking.

Jake unconsciously skimmed his tongue over his own suddenly dry lips. Damn, he had been forced to wage a fierce inner battle to resist the impulse to taste her damp hair and her flushed cheeks and her sweet mouth. Then, when he had lowered his gaze to her body, the impulse had expanded into a need to draw Sarah into his arms. He had experienced a physical ache at the sight of her slender form embraced by that satin robe, which revealed every delectable curve, yet concealed every tantalizing feminine secret.

Becoming uncomfortably warm, Jake lowered the car window all the way, allowing the crisp air access to his overheated flesh. Man, he had it bad, he thought, laughing softly at himself, at his erotically active imagination.

But the funny part was, Jake reflected as he drew the car to a stop at the side of the road near the grade school, Sarah had appeared every bit as appealing and sexy to him after she was fully dressed.

Keeping a sharp eye on the youngsters converging on the school, Jake mulled over the hours he had spent in Sarah's apartment, in an attempt to rationalize and understand the intense attraction he felt for her.

"Good morning, Officer Wolfe!"

The chorused greeting from a group of second grade girls distracted Jake from his introspection.

"Morning, ladies," he responded, as always, eliciting giggles from the girls. "Got your thinking caps on?"

"Oh, yes, sir!" They fairly sang the daily reply.

From there, Jake made the short run to the middle school, where the scene was reenacted—sort of.

"Hi, Jake." The less formal greeting came from a couple of eighth grade boys...who believed they were cool.

"Hi, kids." Jake gave the boys a wave. "Ready to wow the teacher with your superior knowledge?"

"Yeah, right," one boy retorted.

"I wouldn't want to give her a heart attack," the other boy joked.

Jake stuck his head out the window. "Yeah, but it wouldn't hurt to give her a surprise, now and then," he suggested in a muted shout.

Laughing, the boys scuffed along the walk to the entrance doors. Laughing himself, Jake drew his head back inside and once more set the car in motion; it was time to check out the kids arriving at the high school.

The routine never varied whenever Jake was on the day shift, and yet he was continually amazed at how tall and mature the high school kids seemed to be— that is the boys were tall, the girls were mature.

After the last one of the kids—an extra-tall, all-arms-and-legs, gangly basketball player—loped into the low, modern building, Jake felt a surge of adrenaline as he headed the car in the direction of the college campus.

Sarah.

Although Jake knew his chances of seeing Sarah were somewhere between slim and none, he could not contain the expectant tingle that skipped erratically through his body, or the thoughts that danced inside his mind.

What *was* the attraction? Jake mused, automatically cruising the perimeter of the college grounds, keeping a keen, hopeful eye out for a particular woman.

Sarah was good to look at, but, Jake reminded himself, he had known many good-to-look-at women. He had even shared mutually satisfying intimacy with a few of them.

So then, Jake had to surmise that the attraction was therefore more than merely physical.

She was intelligent. It hadn't taken him long to realize and appreciate her sharp mind.

She possessed a quick, rather dry sense of humor; dry, wry wit never failed to capture Jake.

She could cook. While Jake certainly valued culinary expertise, he didn't consider the skill a prerequisite in a woman. When it came to culinary skills, he had heard some testimonials to his own talents.

But, for Jake, she had one outstanding attribute; Sarah Cummings was just plain nice...nice to be around, nice to talk to and, he knew instinctively, nice to make love with.

All things considered, he concluded, Sarah had a lot of plus factors going for her.

The tingle bubbling away inside Jake awakened him to the here, the now and the time. He shot a glance at his watch, and the tingle bubbled over into an eager smile. Smoothly turning the car, he drove away from the campus, heading for the little hamburger joint.

It was five minutes until coffee-break time.

Five minutes until Sarah time.

Jake could hardly wait.

Anxious and excited, he glided the car to a stop inches from the curb in front of the hamburger joint—which bore the ludicrous name The Golden Spatula—just as Sarah crossed the street, in the middle of the block.

"I could cite you, you know," he said as he stepped out of the car, frowning in mock sternness.

"What?" Sarah wasn't wearing the big round glasses. Her soft brown eyes grew wide, and flickered with—fear? "For—for what?" she asked in a quivery voice. She made a misstep and stumbled on the curb.

Jake's quick reflexes saved her from pitching forward and landing on her face on the sidewalk. The minute she was upright and steady again, Sarah pulled her arm free of his grasp and shied away from him.

For crying in a bucket, Jake thought, staring at her in stunned disbelief. What is her problem? Last night, Sarah had relaxed with him, conversed, laughed. Now, suddenly, she appeared as nervous and apprehensive as she had yesterday morning—if not even more so.

"I...I asked you a question," she said, in a dry, crackling voice that was still rife with tension.

Confused by her turnabout, Jake had forgotten her demand for an explanation. What in hell had he said to set her off? He racked his brain, and then the answer hit him. Oh, yeah. He had teased her about a citation. Big deal.

"I was only—" he began, but she cut him off in a tone that contained equal measures of feisty belligerence and edgy trepidation.

"You said you could cite me. For what?"

"Jaywalking," he answered, shaking his head, as if trying to clear his thoughts.

"Jaywalking!" Sarah exclaimed. Now it was her turn to stare at him in disbelief.

"I was teasing you, Sarah." Jake didn't know if he should laugh out loud or curse under his breath. "You crossed in the middle of the block."

"Oh." The fight, and the fear, visibly left Sarah, leaving him relieved but no less confused.

"I need some coffee," he declared, crossing the sidewalk to open the door of the café and hold it for her. "What about you?"

"Yes." Appearing to drag her feet without actually doing so, Sarah joined him at the doorway.

What was she doing here, with him?

Sarah slid into the booth Jake indicated, using the ploy of depositing her books and handbag in the corner of the bench seat as a means of avoiding his probing stare.

Jake probably thought she was some kind of a fool, Sarah reflected. No, he probably thought she was *all* kinds of a fool. Just another flaky woman who couldn't make up her tiny little mind, blowing warm, then cool, friendly, then antipathetic, calm then jumpy.

And Sarah couldn't honestly say she could blame him, if in fact that was Jake's perception of her. Her behavior—yesterday, last night and now—hardly suggested a high level of intelligence.

But there was a difference between last night and this morning; Jake was once again in uniform.

"Oh, hi, Jake, Miss Cummings," Dave called, strolling out of the kitchen. "I didn't hear you folks come in."

"You need a bell over the door," Jake suggested.

"Nah." Dave shook his head. "I tried that when I first opened the place. The damn thing drove me nuts." His shrug conveyed unconcern. "What can I get you? Two coffees?"

"Yes, please," Sarah murmured.

"The same for me," Jake said. Then he added, "And one—no, make it two—of your famous Coney Island hot dogs." He glanced at Sarah. "You want a dog?"

"At ten o'clock in the morning?" Sarah grimaced. "I'll pass, thank you."

Jake's expression dismissed the consideration of time. "Hey, I've been up since five-thirty, and all I've had is a cup of coffee and Mr. Bennet's power cocktail. I'm hungry."

"For a Coney Island hot dog?" She shuddered. "With raw onions and sauce and...everything?"

"Yeah." Jake smacked his lips. "All that good stuff."

"Incredible."

Jake frowned. "What's so incredible about it?"

"Well," Sarah replied, unaware that the tension was slowly easing from her, "I mean, to follow a health drink with a loaded hot dog seems counterproductive."

Jake tossed her a grin born of the devil. "What can I tell you? I'm a junk-food junkie. And my particular favorite happens to be Coney Island hot dogs."

"And cheeseburgers," Dave reminded Jake, coming to a stop at the booth, steaming mugs of coffee in his hands. "Don't forget the cheeseburgers."

"Yeah," Jake said, on an exaggerated sigh. "I love a good cheeseburger. Maybe I'll change my order."

"Too late," Dave informed him, turning away. "I already got your dogs on the grill."

Jake slanted a gleaming glance at Sarah. "Independent bas—son of a gun, isn't he?"

Sarah wanted to remain aloof from Jake, wanted to remain cool, distanced, but she simply couldn't. Despite her genuine apprehension at the thought of any involvement with him, a police officer, she simply couldn't resist. Dismay stabbed at her mind, even as a smile tugged at her lips.

Why did Jake Wolfe have to be so darned nice?

"Come out, come out, wherever you are," Jake sang, chanting the childhood hide-and-seek refrain.

"What?" Sarah blinked herself out of her reverie. "What do you mean?"

"You were hiding inside there," Jake explained, tapping his temple with his forefinger.

"Oh, I was . . . er, just thinking."

"About me?" he asked, brightly, hopefully.

"Certainly not," she lied, and in a reproving tone of voice, at that. Lifting her cup, she took a tentative sip of the aromatic and still hot coffee.

"Oh." Disappointment weighted his tone. "About your problems with your students, then?"

Sarah choked on the coffee. Did he know? The frantic thought flashed through her mind. She had to find out. Catching her breath, she blurted out, "What do you mean?"

"Mean?" Jake gave her a strange look. "Nothing in particular." His dark eyes probed her anxious expression. "I was led to believe," he went on, "that all teachers had problems getting their subject across to at least some of their students. Was I led astray—down the academic path, so to speak?" he asked teasingly.

The wave of relief that washed over Sarah was so forceful it robbed her of breath and speech. Fortunately, at that moment, Dave came up to the booth, bearing a plate containing two hot dogs that smelled positively scrumptious.

"Two Coney Islands," he intoned, sliding the plate onto the table in front of Jake. "Try not to wolf 'em down, as usual, Wolfe." Chuckling to himself at his own play on words, he turned and ambled back behind the counter.

"You're a card, Dave," Jake called after him. "Hopefully by the time you're fifty-two you'll be a full deck."

"Ha!" Dave retorted. "I turned fifty-two six months ago." And although he didn't voice it, his tone said, *So what?* Shrugging, he turned to go back to the kitchen.

"Some character," Jake said, sinking his strong white teeth into the first of the dogs. He chewed the bite, swallowed, then gave an appreciative sigh. "Man, that's good. Sure you don't want the other one?" He arched his dark brows.

"No." Sarah smiled and shook her head. "Thank you. All I want is the coffee."

"You're a cheap date," he murmured, his eyes dancing with a teasing gleam. "I'll keep that in mind when I make reservations for our dinner date."

"Dinner date?" Sarah blinked. "What dinner date?"

Jake was chomping away on his second dog. He washed it down with coffee before answering. "I owe you one."

"No, really, you don't," Sarah insisted, telling herself she absolutely could not see him again.

"A debt's a debt, Miss Cummings," Jake told her in a deep and serious tone. "You took me in when I was hungry. Took pity on me when I was alone and lonely." His somber expression warred with the sparkle in his eyes. "I do owe you one."

He was a police officer, Sarah reminded herself. A cop. She couldn't afford to see him, date him, be with him. He was too attractive, too charming, too damned nice.

"How about this evening?"

"All right." Shocked by the acceptance that blurted from her mouth, Sarah sat staring at him in self-amazement. Where was her mind? Her sense of self-preservation? Jake's steady regard held promise, and an answer. Lost, all lost in the depths of his warm, smiling eyes.

"Good." Jake's satisfied murmur flowed over her like a benediction. "Do you have a food preference? Italian? Chinese? Mexican? Steak and potatoes?"

Decisions, decisions. Sarah felt unequal to the task of choosing. It was a new sensation for her; as a rule, she was decisive, certain, prepared to meet any challenge. Except the one posed by those three male students—and now Jake.

In desperation, Sarah made the only decision she felt capable of making—no decision at all.

"I like all of the above, so I'll leave it to you. You choose the restaurant and the cuisine, please."

"Anyplace?" he asked, as innocent as a soft spring rain.

"Anyplace," she agreed, without thinking.

He pounced. "Okay, my place."

Anyplace but *there*. Sarah opened her mouth to decline, but Jake was quicker to the draw.

"I'll return the favor and cook for you this time."

No. Sarah slowly moved her head from side to side. Being with him in a public restaurant was one thing. Being alone with him, in his place, was out of the question. Again she opened her mouth to decline; again he was quicker.

"I'm a pretty good cook," Jake assured her. "And I promise you won't be disappointed."

That was what Sarah was afraid of, being alone with him, and not being disappointed. Yet, even as she told herself she could not allow the attraction she felt for him to lead her astray, her mind chose to have a mind of its own.

"What time?"

Jake's smile could have melted a polar ice cap. "I go off duty at five. What time are you through for the day?"

"I'm usually finished by three," Sarah replied, unable to believe she was voluntarily falling in line with his plans. Nevertheless, she continued to explain. "But today's Friday, and the head of the history department has a standing end-of-the-week wrap-up meeting every Friday afternoon. I seldom get home before four-thirty."

"Suppose I pick you up at six-thirty?"

"Six-thirty will be fine." Well, she was committed now, Sarah thought—or was it that she *should* be committed? "But it isn't necessary for you to pick me up," she went on, keeping her doubts and uncertainties to herself. "Just give me your address, I can find my way there."

"Uh-uh." Jake shook his head. "I'll come for you, and I'll bring you back home." His voice was edged with hard finality. "This is a quiet town, but I'm not about to take any chances with your safety."

It was a bit ridiculous, maybe even dumb, but Jake's adamant determination instilled in Sarah a pleasant feeling of being cared for and protected. Not that she needed protecting, she hastened to assure herself. She was quite capable of taking care of herself. And yet having Jake so obviously concerned for her well-being gave her a sense of security unlike anything she had ever before experienced. Sarah was touched, and she didn't know quite how to respond.

"Well, all right," she finally said, fully aware she had once again caved in to him. "If you insist."

"I do." Jake's voice was soft; his eyes were softer. "Would you like more coffee?"

"No, thank you. I haven't even fin—" Sarah broke off, her eyes widening as she caught sight of his large watch, and the position of the hands on its face. "Good grief, will you look at the time!" she cried, fumbling for her purse and books. "I've got a class in twenty minutes." Scooping up her things, she slid out of the booth.

"Hey, relax." Jake tossed some bills on the table and followed after her. "I'll run you over to the campus."

"No!" When she heard the note of panic in her voice, Sarah drew a deep, calming breath. "I, ah...I mean, really, I can get there as fast by cutting across the campus."

"Are you sure?" Jake frowned, watching her warily, as if she had suddenly flipped out or something.

Sarah could hardly blame him, but she couldn't explain her seemingly strange behavior. And there was no way she was going to be seen getting out of a patrol car anywhere near the campus. She might be attracted to Jake, but she wasn't stupid.

"Yes," she answered, starting for the door.

"The money for the check is on the table, Dave." Jake called, trailing after her. "See you tomorrow."

"I'll be here," Dave drawled.

"Bye, Dave," Sarah called over her shoulder, pausing to stack her books on one arm as Jake skirted around her to open the door for her.

"Have a good one, folks." Dave's laconic voice drifted to them from the kitchen.

Surely Jake wouldn't use his official vehicle this evening. The dismaying thought occurred to Sarah as she stepped outside and saw the black-and-white police car parked along the curb. No, of course not, she reassured herself. At least she hoped he wouldn't.

"Something wrong?"

"What?" Sarah swung around to stare at him, and nearly dropped the stack of books in the process.

"I asked if there was something wrong." Jake's expression said reams about her odd behavior. "You're looking at the car as if you're afraid it'll attack you."

"That's silly," she said, in what she hoped sounded like a tone of amusement. "I'm distracted, that's all, and I really must rush now." She strode across the pavement.

"Sarah."

Jake's urgent call brought her up short, and she teetered on the curb as she twisted around to face him. "Yes?"

"Careful of the curb," he cautioned. His lips twitched into a smile. "Maybe you should put on your glasses."

As nervous and edgy as she was, Sarah still could not suppress a smile in return. "I can see just fine," she said, loftily. "I only need the glasses for reading."

"Hmm..."

She turned back to the street at the skeptical sound of his murmured response. "Now I really must go."

"Sarah." Jake's lowered voice had the strength to pull her around to face him again.

"Yes?"

"Six-thirty," he said softly. "I can't wait."

The blunt honesty of his admission went directly to her senses, warming her from the inside out. The glow of anticipation in his eyes intensified the warmth, melting the last lingering shreds of her resistance.

"I'll be ready," she whispered, held motionless, as if mesmerized, by the promise in his eyes.

"Get cracking, or you'll be late for class."

Jake's low-voiced command jolted Sarah into awareness, of the time, of where she was, of the depth and power of the effect he had on her senses.

"I'm off," Sarah said, quickly scanning the street before dashing across it. And in more ways than one, she told herself, making a beeline for the campus.

Sarah was panting from her headlong rush by the time she was trotting past the library, two buildings away from her own. Intent on reaching her destination on time, she almost missed seeing the three young men huddled together at the corner of the brick structure.

But something about them drew her attention. Shifting a quick glance at them, she caught her breath. Even without her glasses, Sarah could see that all three of the students had a furtive, highly charged look.

Silence is golden, the tallest of the young men had told her, yet he was anything but silent at that moment. His voice low, his expression strained, Andrew Hollings appeared to be giving orders to the other two students.

". . . and your mouths shut this time," Sarah heard him snarl. Feeling a premonitory shiver of dread, she averted her face and rushed by at an outright run.

What in heaven's name were they involved in? Sarah wondered, not for the first, or even the fifty-first, time. The three had done something, committed some crime, and, judging by the snippet of conversation she had unfortunately overheard last week, it had been some kind of robbery.

But why? The question of motive had nagged at Sarah all week. It didn't make sense. The three young men were all seniors. They were close friends, had been friends for years, long before deciding to attend the same college. They were all from upper-upper-middle-class families, and they shared similar backgrounds. They had all attended excellent schools, and had maintained high scholastic averages throughout their first three years of college.

Dashing into the lecture hall, Sarah was unaware of the greetings called to her by the gathering class. Her thoughts were centered not on her presentation, but on the mystery of the three young men, and their apparent foray into the dangerous territory outside the law.

Sarah addressed the class as usual. "Good morning, ladies and gentleman. Shall we begin?"

While guiding the class through the intricacies of ancient Chinese history, Sarah managed to push her concerns for the three young men to the back of her mind. But the minute the class ended, speculation and worry surged forward into her consciousness again. During her lunch period, her mind gnawed on the mystery as thoroughly as her teeth chewed the food she didn't want or taste.

That the three of them had taken at least one step outside the law was patently evident. Sarah had little doubt on that score. She had heard only bits and pieces of their muttered discussion, but what she had heard was more than enough to convince her and condemn them.

Her memory of the shocking bits and pieces she had heard was clear, sharp, frightening. Most of the comments had been made by two of them, who appeared, paradoxically, both nervous and somewhat cocky.

We pulled it off.

What if we were seen?

Do you believe what they paid us?

I wasn't sure we could do it.

The police . . .

That was the extent of the bits and pieces from the two young men. The comments were suspect, but not conclusive out of context. But it was the harsh, biting remark from Andrew Hollings that had convinced Sarah of their complicity.

If you hang on to your nerve, and keep your mouths shut, we'll be safe from the police.

It was then that Andrew had noticed Sarah, standing in the shadows inside the doors of the lecture hall. He had glared at her with dark, threatening eyes and whispered the warning that continued to revolve inside her mind.

Silence is golden, Miss Cummings.

Three

———

Jake was beginning to feel like he had been waiting for ever for quitting time to come, and for the damn light to turn green at the intersection.

Heaving an impatient sigh, he drummed his blunt fingertips on the steering wheel and shot a glance at his watch. He still had an hour to go. The two-way squawked just as the light finally changed color.

The instructions coming through were for Jake to investigate a reported theft. Responding to directions, he turned at the next intersection and headed out of town.

The scene of the alleged crime was on a property located on the very fringes of his jurisdiction. The house Jake arrived at was set some distance back from the blacktop country road. An expensive bi-level, constructed mainly of wood and natural stone, the place was private, hidden by a stand of screening trees. The man who answered the doorbell was in his early forties, trim, fit and mad as hell.

"I damn well don't believe this," the man raved, glaring at Jake as though he were personally responsible for the situation. "Lord, do you have any idea what it cost me?"

"No, sir," Jake answered, in a professionally calm and soothing tone. "I don't even know what *it* is."

"My car, damn it!" the man shouted, spearing stiff fingers through already ruffled hair. "Come look," he went on, charging past Jake.

Jake dutifully loped after the irate man, nearly crashing into him when he came to an abrupt halt at the open door of a two-car garage.

"Will you just look at that mess?" the man said, in tones of outraged disgust. "Over forty thousand dollars, and they stripped it bare."

They sure had, whoever they were, Jake silently agreed as he stepped inside the garage to view the remains of what had probably once been an impressive-looking luxury car.

Amateurs, he concluded. Professional car thieves wouldn't have taken the time to strip the vehicle, thereby losing the resale value of the leftover parts. Professionals would simply have swiped the car, most likely by running it onto the back of a truck.

"Almost sacrilegious," Jake murmured, in sympathy and understanding of the man's shock and fury. "And the sad part is, the thief or thieves will probably get upwards of fifty, sixty, seventy thousand for the parts."

"Lord!" the man growled. "I could throw up."

No doubt, Jake thought. "I hope you don't," he said in all seriousness. "The sight will make me queasy."

"No kidding?" The man shifted his gaze to Jake, obviously distracted by his admission. "But you're a cop."

"What does that have to do with the price of fish?" Jake asked dryly, stepping into the dim interior of the garage to get a closer look at the pile of debris.

"Well, you know..." The man flicked a hand, as if trying to pluck the answer out of the air. "People like you, cops, firemen, paramedics, you see all kinds of gory stuff—murder victims, people all mangled in highway collisions and such."

"Uh-huh," Jake grunted, kneeling beside the hulk of what had once been an automobile.

"Do those sights make you queasy?"

"Yeah." Jake cocked his head to grin at the man. "Sad, but regrettably true."

"I could never be a cop," the man confessed, grimacing. "I mean, with all the crap you people have to put up with from hoods and badasses—besides all that gory stuff. I guess it takes a certain type of person."

Like stupid? Jake hid a wry smile and kept the observation to himself.

"So, what do you think the chances are of me ever seeing my car parts again?"

Rising, Jake turned to look the man straight in the eyes. "You want an acceptable answer, or the truth, Mr.—" He paused and raised his eyebrows questioningly.

"Hawkins," the man supplied. "Robert Hawkins. And I'm a big boy—I can handle the truth."

"Okay, Mr. Hawkins, from my experience, I'd say your chances are slim to none."

Robert Hawkins sighed and allowed his shoulders to droop. "I suspected as much." He expelled a short humorless laugh. "Boy, the insurance company's gonna love me."

In spades, Jake thought. And higher premiums. But that wasn't his concern, or part of his job description. Get to work, Wolfe, he advised himself, taking a quick look at his watch. *Tempus fugit* and all that.

Sarah.

Excitement coiled deep in Jake's gut, playing hell with his libido, as well as his thought processes. Dragging his thoughts into line, and his notebook from his back pocket, he proceeded with the drill of getting the facts together for his official report.

"When did you discover the theft?"

"Right before I called the station. Three-thirty, quarter to four, somewhere around then," Mr. Hawkins said, shrugging. "Not long after I woke up."

"You work the late shift?"

"Hell, no." Hawkins sounded mildly offended, as if he believed himself too good for anything as plebeian as the graveyard shift. "I'm the personnel manager for the Franklin Container Company in Norristown."

"I see." Jake jotted down the information. "You were home sick from work today?"

"No, no," Hawkins snapped angrily. "What does that have to do with my car being ripped off, anyway?"

"I'm not just being inquisitive, sir." Jake employed a soothing tone. "I'm attempting to ascertain an approximate time when the robbery took place."

"Oh, sorry." Hawkins flushed. "I took a vacation day today."

If one was taking a day, Friday was a good one. Jake kept that opinion to himself, as well. Of course, the information given wasn't a whole lot of help in ascertaining the approximate time of the robbery.

Jake frowned.

Robert Hawkins got the unstated hint, and launched into an explanation. "My lady friend and I left early last evening for Atlantic City, and we didn't get back till around five this morning."

"You have a run of luck?" Jake asked, prepared to offer his congratulations.

"Not really." Hawkins shrugged. "Oh, I won a little, but that wasn't why we stayed so late."

"Hmm . . ." Jake murmured noncommittally. Hell, it wasn't any of his business. Besides, he never gambled, not anymore. He had lost the urge after gorging himself in Vegas during his rebellious, wandering years. He had been to the seaside resort only once, out of curiosity. Still, it sure seemed to him to be a lot of hours to spend in a casino.

"We had tickets for an early show," Hawkins said, apparently reading Jake's expression. "Then we gambled a little. Then we had dinner in one of the swank hotel restaurants. Then we gambled a little more. Then we took in a late show." He shrugged again. "You know how it goes."

"Well, no . . ." Jake admitted. "But I'll take your word for it. Five o'clock, huh?" he mused aloud, bringing the conversation back to the subject. "That leaves eleven or so hours open. . . ."

"And the door," Hawkins inserted, making a face.

Jake arched his brows. "The door?"

"The garage door." Hawkins sighed. "I was beat, all I wanted to do was hit the bed. I forgot to close the garage door."

"It's your property," Jake observed.

"Yeah, damn it!" Hawkins's anger was aroused again. "Just because I forgot to shut the damn door, that doesn't give any two-bit thief the right to waltz in and strip my car, does it?"

"No, sir," Jake said, once again trying for a calming tone. "You'll have to come down to the station to . . ."

"I know, I know," Hawkins cut in impatiently. "Formality, red tape, and I'll bet you a dollar against a slug I'll never see those parts again."

Jake shook his head. "No, sir. No bet. Sorry." He glanced around the area. "It'd be my guess the thief or thieves did the job somewhere in the couple of hours between the time you arrived home and dawn. You're pretty secluded here, but you do have neighbors, and stripping a car isn't the kind of crime usually committed in full daylight."

"I suppose you're right." Hawkins stared at what had been his car less than twelve hours before and heaved a long sigh. "Does that help you at all?"

"Not much," Jake confessed. "But we'll get on it, put it out on the wire."

"Thanks."

Although Robert Hawkins didn't add "for nothing," Jake heard the implied phrase in the man's voice—and the despair. While he sympathized with the man, there wasn't much he could do about it, aside from the routine of asking questions and looking around for possible clues, such as tire tracks left by the vehicle the thief or thieves had used.

There were none. Other than the heap of what was now junk on the garage floor, there was nothing, except Jake's educated guess that the thieves were very likely amateurs—which really wasn't a lot of help, either.

It was past five by the time Jake got to the station, past quitting time, and he still had reports to complete. By the time he got home, it was creeping up on six. He still had to shower, dress and... Jake sighed as he glanced around the living room. He had to straighten up the place.

What in hell was he going to throw together for dinner? The thought struck him, stopped him cold in the process of plumping the throw pillows on the sofa.

Dashing into the kitchen, Jake peered into the freezer. Fate smiled upon him; there were two thick Delmonico steaks, a package of frozen Idaho baked potatoes, and a frozen warm-and-serve apple pie—almost like homemade.

The liquor cabinet revealed a bottle of cabernet sauvignon, which he slid onto a rack in the fridge. At least the sink wasn't cluttered with dishes, since he hadn't bothered preparing breakfast that morning.

Jake shot a look at his watch, cursed and took off for the bathroom. He nearly scalded himself by stepping under the shower before adjusting the water temperature, and he nicked himself three times while scraping the beard shadow from his face. In between pulling on blue socks, darker blue pants and a lighter-blue-and-white striped shirt, and hop-stepping into black leather slip-ons, he tugged the covers neatly into place on the still-rumpled unmade bed.

Sarah.

A sensuous thrill arrowed through Jake's body.

A man could always dream.

Jake smiled in self-mockery as he shrugged into a navy Windbreaker, took another quick, longing look at the bed, then loped out of the apartment at six-twenty.

There was no law on the books against wishful thinking.

A man was entitled to his fantasies.

Was she completely crazy, or what?

Sarah tugged the brush through her hair and grimaced, both at the sharp pain in her scalp and at the question repeating itself inside her head.

Had she actually agreed to have dinner alone with a man in his apartment?

Yes, she had.

Crazy, or dumb or both.

Even now, hours later, Sarah couldn't believe she had capitulated so easily. And it wasn't just that Jake Wolfe was a virtual stranger to her, an unknown quantity... *He was a police officer, for heaven's sake.*

But he was such a nice police officer, Sarah defended herself. And, with his tall, long-muscled body, he did look fantastic in that uniform, she allowed, turning away from the dresser mirror to cross the bedroom to the clothes closet. And he was so strikingly good-looking, she reflected, staring dejectedly at the selection of garments draped on satin hangers looped over the metal rod.

And she had nothing glamorous to wear.

That errant, wailing thought startled Sarah out of her moody introspection.

Glamorous? Sarah frowned. The word *glamorous* connoted romance and excitement. She certainly was not looking for either of those things.

Who was she kidding? Sarah pulled a sand-washed silk dress in a forest-green, rust-and-gold pattern from the rod. All Jake had to do was glance at her with his deep, dark blue eyes and she got excited.

And mush-minded with thoughts of romance.

Her sigh whispered in the quiet room. A sigh born of dismay and anxiety. She couldn't take a chance on getting involved with Jake, or even be too friendly with him. She had seen the threat in Andrew Hollings's eyes when he had warned her to keep silent. His threat had not been an empty one. If she was seen in public with Jake, if her name was linked with his, Andrew would soon hear about it, and act on it.

Sarah shivered. Andrew had never appeared sinister or capable of violence. Nor had either one of the other two young men. They were all so bright, always well-mannered and pleasant.

What had they gotten themselves into to cause such a radical change in their personalities?

That their recent extracurricular activities had been illegal, Sarah had little doubt. She had heard enough of their discussion to convince her of their complicity, and some inner sense told her that none of them would hesitate to silence her if she gave any indication of voicing her suspicions—and most especially Andrew of the threatening tone and eyes.

Sarah sighed again, feeling trapped and frustrated. Jake looked to be the best thing to come her way in— Damn, she had never in her adult life met any man halfway as interesting and exciting as Jake. Why had she met him now? she thought in protest against the lousy timing of destiny. At any other time, in any other place...

Yet another, heavier sigh broke the silence.

Dragging her thoughts away from the edge of depression, Sarah slipped her feet into rust-colored suede heels and turned to leave the bedroom.

It was not another time or place, and she would have to deal with that fact. Jake was now and here and—

The doorbell rang.

Sarah froze in the bedroom doorway.

Jake was *here*.

A stab of sheer panic immobilized her for a moment, but then she raised her chin, squared her shoulders and crossed the living room to open the door. Her breath caught, lodged in her throat, at the sight of him.

Jake Wolfe looked devastating in navy blue.

"Hi."

His smile didn't exactly lack impact, either. She felt the blow to the tips of her tingling toes.

"Hi." Sarah could barely articulate the tiny word.

"You look beautiful." His bone-melting eyes made a slow survey of her body.

Sarah's bones dutifully melted. "Thank you." Lord, did that reedy little voice belong to her? "You . . . you're looking rather terrific yourself."

Jake's eyes softened.

Sarah's insides liquified.

"Ready?"

For anything you might suggest. Hearing the yearning note in her silent reply, Sarah snapped herself back to reality. There was no longer any doubt in her mind; she *was* crazy.

"Yes," she said, reluctantly taking her gaze from him to turn away. "Let me get my purse and coat."

Jake moved into the room to help her with her coat. Sarah immediately wished he hadn't played the gentleman. The touch of his long, strong fingers on her shoulders, at her nape, sent a fiery shower of sensations cascading throughout her being, and ignited a smoldering spark in the core of her femininity. Feeling seared all over, she stepped away from temptation.

"What's for dinner?" she asked, too brightly. "I'm starving." She smiled, too brilliantly.

"Er . . . well . . ." Jake followed her into the hallway and stood to one side as she shut and locked the door. "I wanted to cook one of my special dishes for you, but I was running late and . . ." He paused to give her a self-deprecating, and thoroughly captivating, smile. "How do you feel about steak and baked potatoes?"

"I love steak and baked potatoes." Sarah frowned, and concentrated on descending the narrow, rather steep stairs. "Why? I mean, since I had a vegetable dish yesterday, and didn't want a hot dog this morning, were you thinking I was a confirmed vegetarian?" She tossed a quizzical glance at him.

"Something like that," Jake admitted, obviously relieved. He stepped around her to open the door. "I'm glad to hear you're not antimeat, especially red meat."

"Not anti, at least, not entirely," Sarah said as she walked past him. "But, in reaction to all the adverse publicity on it, I have cut down on my consumption of meat in the last few years."

"You know," Jake mused, trailing her outside and down the three shallow steps to the pavement. "I sometimes question the benefits of all the instant media communications we are bombarded with today."

"Are you implying that ignorance is bliss?" Sarah asked teasingly, while absorbing a wave of relief at the absence of a black-and-white police car along the quiet street.

"Yeah, I suppose I am." Grinning at her, Jake crossed the sidewalk to a smart-looking silver-and-gray sedan. "But, to use another old saying, maybe a little knowledge is a dangerous thing."

Ignorance is bliss. A little knowledge is a dangerous thing. Sarah felt chilled, struck by the truth of the maxims as they related to her own situation with regard to Andrew Hollings and the other two men.

A little knowledge concerning their apparently ne-
farious activities had robbed her of her own blissful
ignorance, and placed her in danger.

Murmuring an absent "Thank you," Sarah slid into
the car, then sat staring through the windshield, con-
templating her precarious position, as Jake shut the
door and circled around to the driver's side.

"Buckle up."

His soft command defused the flash of panic flaring to life inside Sarah. With breathtaking sudden-
ness, she was struck by the realization that just
knowing Jake was there, close by, gave her an intense
feeling of security and protection.

But was it the presence of the man, or the police
officer? Obeying orders, Sarah fastened the belt, and
slanted a sidelong look and a tentative smile at him.

"What?" Jake's hands stilled in the act of con-
necting his own seat belt, a curious smile kicking up
the corners of his well-defined mouth.

Should she take a chance and confide in him? Staring into his puzzled eyes, barely aware that he had
spoken, Sarah toyed with the idea of dumping her
worries, her fears, onto his broad, powerful-looking
shoulders.

"Sarah?"

Ensnared in the morass of her own thoughts, Sarah
continued to stare at him, weighing the pros and cons
of revealing to him her suspicions about the three students.

On the pro side was Jake himself, tall, strong, exuding a palpable aura of capability and confidence. While on the side of the cons was the irrefutable fact that Sarah had no real evidence to present to him. There were the disjointed bits and pieces of conversation she had overheard, and her intuitive certainty, but she possessed no proof at all.

Silence is golden, Miss Cummings.

What, she wondered, would Jake make of Andrew's threatening advice to her? Then again, what *could* he make of it, when for all intents and purposes Andrew had merely cited yet another tried and true axiom?

"Sarah, honey, what's wrong?" Jake's voice wore a sharp edge of concern that cut through the gridlock of her converging thoughts.

"Nothing . . . I . . ." Sarah paused to gather her wits and find a plausible excuse for her distraction; unconsciously her decision had been reached. Rather than involve Jake, and possibly place him in danger, too, she would adhere to Andrew's dictum and remain silent.

Jake's eyes narrowed. "There's something. You look so . . . strained, almost frightened." He released the belt, and it snapped back into position, forgotten as he leaned across to stare deep into her eyes. "You're not afraid of being alone with me in my apartment, are you?"

"Oh, no," Sarah said at once, at that moment realizing she spoke the truth. "I was just thinking . . ."

she began, searching for an explanation for her odd behavior. Then her eyes flickered and grew wide as another, equally compelling realization sank in. "You called me honey."

The tension around Jake's eyes and mouth eased visibly. His lips quirked in amusement. "Yes, I did."

"Why?" Sarah asked ingenuously.

The quirk on his lips grew into a beguiling smile. "Because you are one," he said with quiet simplicity. "A real honey of a woman."

"Oh." Sarah was nonplussed. For a woman who disdained the current free-and-easy use of endearments, she felt an inordinate sense of pleasure.

Stretching his long body, Jake leaned closer to her. "Do you mind?" His warm breath caressed her cheek, sending ripples of response through her in ever-widening circles.

Sarah shivered; the feeling was delicious. "N—no..." She shook her head, and stopped breathing. Her action brought her lips to within a wish of his.

"May I taste?" Jake's voice was low, uneven.

Sarah's draining mind grappled with his request for a second, and then understanding spawned excitement. "Here?"

"Just a taste," he murmured, bathing her mouth and her senses with his breath. "An appetizer."

Sarah couldn't speak, couldn't think. All she was capable of was feeling—and, boy, was she feeling. Wild sensations skittered through her body and danced on the surface of her flesh. Her lips burned, her tongue tingled, her meager defenses collapsed.

"Yes, an appetizer, please."

Jake sighed; Sarah felt it in the depths of her being. His mouth brushed hers; she parted her lips. Accepting the silent invitation, he fused his mouth to hers.

Contact. Instant electricity. Sarah felt the charge in every cell and atom in her body. Jake didn't deepen the kiss; he didn't need to apply pressure to fuel the spark. The flame leaped higher and higher.

It was too hot, too combustible, too soon.

Cursing under his breath, Jake pulled back, all the way back to the driver's side, behind the wheel.

Stunned by the magnitude of the unique experience, still quivering in reaction, Sarah stared at him in mute wonder, and slowly raised her fingertips to her sensitized and trembling lips.

"We've got to get out of here." His voice was harsh, raw. "Lord, if Cal had cruised past the car just then, he'd have probably hauled us in and booked us for inflammatory and indecent public behavior."

"Cal?" Sarah blinked and let her hand drop unnoticed into her lap.

Jake drew a deep breath. "Cal Parker, the officer on second-shift patrol." He reached over his shoulder, yanked the seat belt across his body and fumbled with the lock, the fine tremor in his fingers forcing him to make three stabs with the prong before securing it.

"I see." Sarah swallowed; it wasn't easy.

He fired the engine and shot her a piercing look. "Are you all right, honey?"

"Yes." She managed a convincing smile.

"Ready for bland old steak and potatoes?"

"I'll be satisfied with a bland dinner." A teasing imp invaded her mind, and laughed at him out of her eyes. "Because you do serve up one spicy appetizer."

The rich sound of his delighted laughter filled the car, and every nook and cranny of Sarah's heart.

Four

———

A kiss, just a kiss, and not even a very long or deep or intense kiss, at that. There had been no hot possession, no urgent pressure, no dueling tongues.

Just a kiss.

Uh-huh. It was just a kiss, all right, Sarah reflected. Just a kiss that registered 9.5 on her personal quake-measuring scale.

Heavens, over two hours had elapsed since that kiss, and she still felt the inner shocks and tremors. Two hours. Sarah flicked a quick glance at the man seated opposite her at the glass-topped dining table.

Surprisingly, the seconds and minutes of the previous two hours had flowed together smoothly, despite a strong, if unacknowledged, undercurrent of tension.

Sarah and Jake had worked together in outward compatibility and congeniality, chatting and laughing while preparing the meal and setting the table in the cozy dining alcove set off the kitchen. Yet, beneath their surface camaraderie, the tension had remained constant—not a sizzling, frizz-your-hair charge, but more a humming portent of promise.

There had been moments, moments fraught with inherent danger, moments when their arms had brushed, their fingers had touched, their eyes had met and clung.

The signs indicated the potential for another emotional quake—the big one. Sarah sensed it building in the shivery feeling inside her.

She was hiding it well, though, she assured herself, sighing in repletion as she placed her napkin on the table next to her plate.

"For a makeshift, rushed-together meal," she said, smiling across the table at Jake, "that was delicious."

"The pie didn't live up to its claim." Returning her smile, he picked up the wine bottle and topped off their glasses, champagne flutes he had produced for the occasion. "It didn't taste homemade to me—at least, not anywhere near my mother's apple pie."

"I wouldn't know the difference," Sarah admitted, laughing. "My mother is a disaster in the kitchen. My father always teased her by maintaining that she was the only cook he knew who could burn water."

Laughing along with her, Jake slid back his chair and stood. "Let's go into the living room and get comfortable," he said, picking up both glasses.

"After I clear the table," she said, standing and immediately reaching for the empty plates.

Jake stopped her by curling his fingers around her wrist. "That'll wait." He dismissed the clutter with a shrug. "After you." Releasing her wrist, he indicated the living room with a sweeping wave of his arm. "I want to hear more."

"About my mother's cooking?" Unobtrusively rubbing the tingling skin where his fingers had circled her wrist, Sarah preceded him into the living room. "What's to tell?" she asked, grinning, as she settled into the corner of a long sofa. "It's lousy."

"Okay." Jake handed a glass to her, then settled himself on the plump cushion next to hers. "Then I guess I'll have to be content with your life story."

"My entire life story?" Sarah blinked in feigned surprise. "From day one?"

"Every detail," Jake insisted. "From day one, up to yesterday morning."

When we met. He didn't say it; he didn't have to. Sarah instinctively felt the importance he attached to the occasion of their first meeting.

"You're tired?" she asked, with an ease she was light years away from feeling.

"Tired?" Jake frowned. "No. Why?"

"My life story is boring fare," she explained. "Put you to sleep in no time."

"Boring, huh?" Jake's casual tone concealed the baited snare. "Even the steamy, sexy parts?"

Sarah walked into his trap without a thought. "There are no steamy, sexy parts."

A lazy smile sauntered across his lips. "Too bad." His voice held purring satisfaction. He raised his glass to take a sip of the wine, then raised his eyes to gaze into hers. "You want to add some? I'm willing to oblige."

He was teasing her, Sarah assured herself, taking a quick sip of her own wine to wet her suddenly parched mouth and throat. Well, two could play at that game.

"What did you have in mind?" she asked, in tones she hoped sounded blasé and world-weary.

"Getting naked in a tub filled with champagne," he suggested in a sexy drawl.

"Expensive." Sarah managed to maintain her cool composure, despite the bubble of laughter tickling the back of her throat. "Or do you have the wine on hand?"

"No." Jake appeared crestfallen.

"Well, then, I guess you'll have to settle for my life story, dull as it may be."

"Would you consider a bubble bath instead?" he asked hopefully. "I think I have some of that."

"No." Sarah shook her head. "Sorry, it's champagne or nothing."

Jake exhaled a long sigh. "You're a hard woman, Sarah." He paused. "Well, you're not physically hard. Your skin is soft and smooth and—"

Sarah interrupted him ruthlessly. "Do you want to hear my story or not?"

"Lay it on me." Jake flashed her a grin.

Fighting the dazzling effects of it, of him, on her uncertain senses, Sarah launched into a rapid-fire account of her existence prior to their first meeting.

"As I said previously, I'm from Baltimore. I was born and raised there, twenty-seven years ago. My father was and still is a structural engineer, in an upper-management position. My mother is a high school guidance counselor. I was always bookish, living in the historical past, keeping to myself, rather than joining in outside activities." Sarah paused in her narrative to take a sip of wine.

"No siblings...brothers, sisters?" Jake inserted into the lull.

Sarah shook her head. "No, I wish I did. I'd have loved a sister or an older brother, but..." She shrugged.

"That's a shame," he said in commiseration. "I have three—brothers." He laughed softly in reminiscence. "It got wild at times, but never dull."

"I envy you," she said wistfully. "Our house was always quiet. I got lonesome at times."

"No friends?" Jake raised his eyebrows.

"Of course I had friends." Sarah laughed. "Every one as bookish as I, a cadre of overachievers."

"Boyfriends?" he asked pointedly.

"A few," she admitted. "But nothing serious, un-til..." Catching herself, she let her voice fade away to nothing.

"Until?" Jake probed with intent.

Sarah hesitated, loath to talk about the single most uncomfortable and humiliating experience of her otherwise prosaic, uneventful life.

"That bad, huh?" Jake had the look of a dog with a bone firmly clamped in his teeth, a bone he would not relinquish without a struggle.

Stalling for time, Sarah took another long sip of her wine. In retrospect, and from a more mature perspective, the incident, though traumatic at the time, had diminished in significance. She had played the fool, but then, playing the fool was part of the rite of passage into maturity.

Jake decided the issue for her. "You fell in love?" he guessed, accurately.

"Yes," Sarah admitted with a wry smile. "And proceeded to make a fool of myself over the man."

"Big hunk on campus?"

"Oh, no. No half measures for me." Sarah grimaced. "I went the whole nine yards, falling for a professor—the head of the history department, no less."

"Who else?" Jake murmured. "And he made it known that he wasn't interested?"

"He was *very* interested. He was also very married. He let slip enticing little tidbits of information, such as how unhappy and lonely he was, hinting at a pending divorce." She sighed. "I lapped up every word."

"You . . . er, got involved?"

"Involved?" Sarah laughed; it had more the sound of a derisive snort. "*Involved* hardly describes it. For all intents and purposes, I literally worshiped him. He was willing to take anything I offered him. And, in my innocence—or stupidity—I eagerly gave him everything."

Except for a slight tightening of his lips, Jake betrayed no reaction to her blunt recount. His expression remained attentive, but seemingly unaffected. "And when you realized he was using you, you crept away to lick your wounds," he murmured, not in question, but in speculation.

"Oh, no." Sarah bit down on her lip before producing a patently false, overbright smile. "Not I, Miss All-Brains-and-No-Sense. I clung like a limpet." She blinked, glanced away, then turned to look directly at him. "It took a visit from his wife before I finally got the message."

"You loved him?"

"Yes," Sarah whispered. "With all the dramatic fervor only the very young can agonize over."

Jake gazed at her in contemplation for several long moments. "You're still hurting from the experience," he finally said, in a musing tone of voice, as if he were thinking out loud. "And still in love with him. Aren't you?"

His observation startled her. It shouldn't have, Sarah acknowledged. The pain, the humiliation, the self-condemnation she believed she had put behind her still festered deep inside her, hidden, but there. The realization, while enlightening, cast a sobering, unflattering light on her self-image.

"You don't have to answer," Jake said, setting his glass on the floor, then raising his hand to weave his long fingers through hers. "I had no right to ask."

Strangely comforted by the strength of his hand curled around hers, Sarah gave him a weak smile and a quick shake of her head. "It's all right. It was the logical next question. But your conclusion was wrong. Although I must admit to still feeling a residue of the pain and humiliation I inflicted upon myself, I am not still in love with him." She moved her shoulders in a parody of a careless shrug. "In fact, now, from a distance of several years, I realize I never was in love with him."

"Or any other man," Jake concluded.

"Or any other man," she concurred.

"Do you now hate all men?" His voice was low, intense, with a fine edge of concern.

"Hate?" Sarah echoed in surprise. "No, of course not. I'm not so simpleminded as to blame the entire male species for what, in effect, I did to myself. Besides, hate is such a debilitating, pointless emotion, isn't it?"

"Pretty much so," Jake agreed, stroking his fingers down the length of hers. "But," he went on, "I'm certain that there are some, maybe many, who would have taken refuge from self-condemnation by blaming and hating the entire world." He released her fingers to glide his hand up her arm.

Sarah suppressed a responsive gasp, but lost the battle against a receptive shiver. "You—" She had to pause to catch her breath and swallow. "You are very wise," she told him, in a small, trembly voice.

Jake smiled, and trailed his fingers along her shoulder to the side of her neck. "I've been around the block a few times." His index finger stroked the skin above her collar.

Sarah was finding it extremely difficult to breathe. "In...in connection with your police work?" Her voice had been reduced to a reedy murmur.

"Mmm-hmm..." Jake nodded, and shifted from the center cushion to the edge of hers. He leaned into her, so close she could feel his taut muscles, the heat from his body. "The police work," he murmured, prickling her ear and her senses with his warm breath. "And the rawness of life I experienced during my footloose years wandering around the country."

Rawness defined the sensation inside her. The fleeting thought flashed in Sarah's mind, then was gone. Feelings took over, feelings caused by the feather-light touch of Jake's lips against the sensitized skin behind her ear, feelings generated by the glide of his tongue from her ear to her jaw, feelings heightened by the movement of his mouth from her jaw to her trembling lips, and deeper feelings, hot and intense, ignited by the way her mouth was captured beneath the pressure of his lips.

Clinging to her last vestiges of lucidity, Sarah pressed her head back against the sofa, freeing her lips. "I ... ah ... Jake," she panted, tearing her gaze from the alluring flame flaring in his blue eyes to stare numbly at the tremor in the glass in her hand. "I'm afraid my wine's sloshing onto the floor."

"Easily remedied." Levering his torso over hers, he plucked the glass from her hand and set it on the end table next to the sofa. "There." Instead of moving back, beside her, he stretched out his long body the full length of hers.

He was lying on top of her! Sarah felt the weight of his broad chest against her breasts, the nudge of his hips against her pelvis, the bunched-muscle pressure of his long legs against her thighs, and the hard urgency of his ...

Sarah shuddered in response to the flare of moist heat radiating throughout her being from the core of her femininity. Then his mouth brushed hers, and the heat expanded, flowing like molten lava through her veins.

"Now, where were we?" Jake murmured against her lips, filling her mouth, her senses, with his warm, intoxicating, wine-scented breath.

En route to mindlessness? Sarah couldn't articulate the reply that zapped through her surrendering consciousness. It didn't matter; Jake knew precisely where they were, where they were heading and exactly how to get there.

His lips settled on hers. Close, they were getting close. He slanted his mouth, moving his lips to part hers. Closer. The tip of his tongue made a tentative probe. Closer still. Then his tongue speared into her mouth at the same instant his hand covered her breast.

Destination attained.

Sarah's mind shut down. Sensations ruled. And the sensations were all-consuming. The inner heat intensified, sending a shivering thrill up her spine, then down again, back into the depths of her feminine being. Jake's mouth was hard, his searching tongue insistent, demanding a response from her, a response she was beyond denying him. While his tongue engaged hers in rough, erotic play, she raised her arms and coiled them around his taut neck, arching herself up, into him. An exciting, low groan rumbled in his throat. His hand flexed around her breast; his fingers were gentle, teasing, tormenting the tip of her breast into tight arousal, enticing a muffled gasp from her throat.

Sarah's stomach quaked.

The big one?

The fearful thought fought its way through the sensuous fog clouding her gray matter. Too soon, too soon, a faint inner voice warned. Understanding struggled to be born.

Stop him. Sarah heard the shrill inner command and forced her languid limbs to obey. With her dwindling resources of strength, she slid her hands down and pressed against his chest, moving him back, away from her.

"Jake...please..." she pleaded between gasps for breath. "You're moving too fast for me."

To his credit, Jake didn't persist. His chest heaving, his eyes dark and glittery, mirroring the extent of his passion, he flung himself back, away from physical contact with her. Half reclining, the rigidity of his body blatantly displayed the power and potency of his arousal.

As if pulled by an irresistible magnetic force field, Sarah's eyes were drawn to his sprawling figure. Her stomach muscles contracted at the sight of the fiery desire blazing from his eyes, the tightness of his clenched jaw, the lines of strain bracketing his compressed mouth, the quiver in the taut muscles in his legs, and the bulge at the apex of...

Sarah dragged her gaze away from temptation, and propelled herself forcefully from the sofa. "It's...uh, getting late," she said, in a squeaky, breathless voice. "I'll...er...I'll clear the table," she offered, making a beeline for the comparative safety of the dining alcove.

Jake didn't make a move to follow Sarah. In truth, he seriously doubted his ability to pursue her at that moment. He hurt, in the most vulnerable part of his body; the pain was not altogether unpleasant.

Drawing deep, calming breaths into his tight chest, he gazed down the length of his body, following the route Sarah's widened eyes had traversed moments ago.

A wry smile twitched his lips as his gaze came to rest on the full and obvious evidence of the cause of her precipitate flight.

He was hard as cast iron. Jake expelled a rueful chuckle at his apt comparison. He wanted to cast his iron, longed to cast his iron, was damn near perishing from the need to cast his iron, but his target had fled, leaving in her wake a very hard and very uncomfortable man.

He didn't blame her for fleeing. Her protest was valid; he had moved on her too soon, too fast.

At any other time, with any other woman, Jake might have rationalized his impetuous, unconsidered actions. He might have excused himself by citing the temptations Sarah presented—the allure of her body, so excitingly concealed, yet revealed, by that clinging silk dress, the sweet, moist appeal of her soft, full lips, the power of her initial melting response. But none of the excuses were valid, and he knew it. Sarah had not teased or deliberately tempted him. He knew that, as well.

It was hardly Sarah's fault that he couldn't seem to keep his hands, his body, his mind, off her, he admitted, still tingling, aching from the touch and taste of her.

On reflection, the swiftness and the uncommon strength of his arousal gave Jake pause. The experience was unique, he mused, a benchmark in his per-

sonal experience. Not even during his hot and
overeager teenage years had his body risen to the occasion so quickly, so to speak.

Of course, he had been enduring a long dry spell
lately, he reminded himself. It had been some months
since he had been with a woman in an intimate way—
ever since he had returned to Sprucewood, as a matter of fact. But he had gone through dry spells before,
periods lasting even longer than this current span, and
yet when offered the opportunity to end the dry spell,
he had never sprung to full, throbbing life as rapidly,
as urgently, as he had moments ago with Sarah.

Passing strange, Jake decided, frowning as he con-
templated his pulsating state of disappointment. Even
now, when the wind called Sarah had changed course
and was blowing in the direction of the dining alcove,
the sails of his libido remained in unfurled and burst-
ing fullness.

Jake's rueful chuckle erupted in soft laughter.
Damned if he wasn't thinking in allegorical terms,
when he should be applying deductive reasoning to the
mystery. He was a cop, wasn't he? he chided himself,
sighing in relief as his body finally began to relax. So
do your cop thing, he thought—examine the evidence
and draw a conclusion.

Jake cocked his head as the sound of rattling dishes
and cutlery assailed his ears. While he waited out the
slow descent from an unprecedented sexual high,
Sarah was keeping busy, working off her reactions to
it by clearing the table of the remains of their meal.

Sarah.

Jake sighed and surged to his feet. The answer to his physical dilemma didn't require the deductive reasoning of a master sleuth, after all. Bending, he picked up his wineglass from the floor, then collected Sarah's glass from the end table. The answer was contained within her name.

Jake knew with sudden clarity that his instantaneous arousal had been fired by the woman Sarah, and not by a need for transient release with just any woman.

It was a scary concept. A self-confident smile playing over his lips, Jake sauntered across the living room. Lucky for him that he was a cop, a bona fide officer of the law, trained to deal with scary concepts.

The table was cleared, and the dining room was empty. Following the sound of running water, Jake continued on to the archway that led into the kitchen. Sarah stood at the sink, her back to him, her arms submerged in soapy water.

"You shouldn't be doing that," he said, hesitating in the archway. "You had kitchen duty last night."

"I don't mind." Her shoulders moved in a slight shrug. "I'm used to it." Her hands stilled in the act of rinsing a plate. "Are you all right?" Her voice was low, so soft that he could barely hear it over the running water.

"I think I'll live."

Sarah slanted a quick look at him over her shoulder. "Jake, I'm sorry, but I . . ."

"I know," he inserted, trying to make it easier for her. "Not your fault, anyway," he admitted. "I pushed, and I deserved to be shoved back." He waited, and when she didn't reply, he crossed the room to stand next to her, close, but not too close. "I brought your wine." He held the glass up for her to see, then set it on the counter alongside the draining rack.

Sarah gave him a tentative smile. "I think I've had enough wine . . . more than enough."

"It wasn't the wine, Sarah," Jake said decisively, setting his glass next to hers before turning to face her fully. "And you know it as well as I do."

"No, it wasn't the wine," she whispered, lowering her eyes to avoid his piercing stare.

"Look at me, Sarah." Though he kept his voice soft, even, he injected a hint of command into his tone.

Sarah's head snapped up, as if yanked by a cord. She sank her teeth into her lower lip, but held his steady regard.

"There's a strong attraction at play here, physical and emotional. I know it, and you know it." He kept her pinned with his eyes. "Don't you?"

Sarah sighed, "Yes."

"Yes." Jake nodded. "I like being with you, and I believe you like being with me. Am I right?"

"Yes."

"Okay." Jake drew a breath, then threw caution to the winds. "I'll level with you. I want to go to bed with you." He shook his head, sharply, decisively. "No, I don't just want to go to bed with you, I want to submerge myself in you. I want it so damn bad my back teeth ache." He drew another, deeper breath. "But I swear I won't push you again. I'll wait until you tell me, openly, honestly, that you want it, too." He gave her a crooked grin. "It won't be easy...but I'll wait."

"Jake...I..." Her beautiful eyes grew misty with tears; they were nearly his undoing.

"Damn it, Sarah, don't cry, or I'll have to take you in my arms again, hold you close, feel your sexy body beneath that silky material and—" He broke off, stepped back and, turning, pulled a cabinet drawer open and groped inside for a tea towel. "Er...you finish washing. I'll dry."

"All right." Sarah laughed, and sniffed. "And while you're at it, you can tell me *your* life story."

Five

"I came into this world as the clock struck midnight in the clapboard shack on the wrong side of the Reading Railroad tracks."

Struck midnight? Clapboard shack! Sopping dishrag in hand, Sarah forgot the glass she was in the process of washing and turned to frown at the storyteller.

Jake's expression was bland, innocent...deceptively innocent. His eyes, though, looked guilty as hell.

"Go on," she urged, giving him a wry, if not patently disbelieving, smile.

"It was a dark and stormy night..."

Sarah rolled her eyes.

"Well, it was." The twitch of Jake's lips belied his injured tone. "Cold, too."

"Uh-huh." Sarah fought back a giggle. "Continue."

"Outside the wind vas blowing . . . a pushcart filled mit snow?" Jake went on, in a heavily laid-on Pennsylvania Dutch accent, quoting a bit from *Dangerous Dan McGrew,* out of context and, she suspected, incorrectly.

Sarah lost it. Unmindful of the sodden rag she held, she brought her hand up to her mouth to muffle a burst of laughter, and proceeded to go into a fit of choking and gasping at the taste of dish detergent on her tongue.

"Serves you right," Jake said smugly, nevertheless nudging her aside to pour a glass of water for her to cleanse her mouth with. "It's what you get for doubting me."

"I do humbly beg your pardon," Sarah replied, grimacing at the aftertaste of detergent-tainted water.

"And rightly so," Jake retorted reprovingly. Then he ruined the effect by asking, anxiously, "Are you okay?"

"Yes," she assured him with a smile. "But how about something to wash away this awful taste?"

"Your wine?" Jake started to turn toward where he had set the glasses.

Sarah halted his movement by grasping his arm. "No, no more wine. Really, I've had enough."

"A soft drink?" he suggested, turning back to her. "Juice? Tea? Coffee?"

"Do you have decaffeinated coffee?"

"Sure." Jake was moving to the automatic drip machine as he answered. "I'll get it started."

"And while it drips through, I'll finish up here," Sarah offered, plunging her hands into the sink once more.

Fifteen minutes later, the kitchen chores completed, Sarah and Jake were back in the living room, this time seated in separate chairs flanking the window facing the street.

"Okay, you had your fun, and you eased the tense situation with your comedy routine," Sarah said, letting him know she was aware of his earlier intent. She blew on the steaming liquid in the cup cradled in her hands and arched her eyebrows. "Now, are you ready to tell me a little about yourself?"

"You really want to hear about it?" Jake managed to look skeptical and hopeful at one and the same time.

"Yeth, I weally weally do," Sarah insisted, in an impassioned Elmer Fudd impression.

This time Jake lost it, erupting with a roar of appreciative laughter. "As I believe I might have mentioned, I like being with you, Sarah Cummings," he said after the bout of laughter subsided. "I also do believe you show signs of possessing a sense of humor as off-the-wall as my own."

"Do tell," she drawled, concealing the jolt of surprise dealt to her by the startling truth of his observation. Though quiet in appearance and demeanor, she always had possessed an appreciation for the ridiculous. Perhaps it derived from her study of the human foibles history was peppered with. Whatever, along with a strong physical attraction, and a genuine liking for each other, they shared a similar sense of humor.

"I just did," Jake replied, effectively ending her flit into introspection.

"Did what?" Sarah asked, having lost the conversational thread.

"Tell." Jake grinned.

Sarah heaved an exaggerated sigh. "Why do I have this sensation of going in circles?" Since the question was rhetorical, she didn't wait for a response, but plowed on, "Will you get on with it?"

"You're a har—" Jake broke off to shake his head. "I already said that, didn't I?" She nodded; he laughed. "Okay, I'll make it brief."

Sarah glanced at her watch. "Good. Time and tide...and all that jazz."

Jake laughed again. "God, we are trite, if nothing else." He frowned, collecting himself. "Now, where was I?"

"In a shack by the railroad tracks."

"Yeah, well," he grinned. "Actually, I was born right here in Sprucewood, thirty years ago this past summer. I was the youngest of four sons...and spoiled rotten.''

"You were a terror?''

Jake grimaced and nodded. "And rebellious." He shrugged. "Being the last, and with three older brothers who excelled, most especially the eldest brother, I guess I felt that I had to make my own statement, be different.''

"In what way?'' Sarah frowned. "Different from whom—or from what?''

"The family tradition," Jake intoned in a deep voice. "You see, I come from a family of law-enforcement officers, stretching back over a hundred years." He chuckled. "I'm about convinced that the dedication to the law must be in the Wolfe genes or something. Hell, we've had sheriffs, deputies, U.S. marshals—you name it, we've had at least one.''

"That's incredible." Sarah was genuinely fascinated by the idea, both as a person and as a historian. "Over a hundred years, and the tradition is ongoing?''

"Yeah. Anyway, my father was a member of the Philadelphia police force.''

"But he lived here, in Sprucewood?''

"Mmm-hmm..." A faint, sad smile shadowed his lips. "He was originally from Philly. My mother was from Sprucewood. They met, fell in love and got married. They lived in an apartment in the city until my mother got pregnant, and then they decided to settle here to raise a family.''

"And your brothers?" Sarah asked. "They're also in law enforcement?"

"Yes, but not here." Jake smiled. "The third son, Eric, is thirty-three. He followed my father into the Philadelphia police force. Right now he's assigned to the narcotics division, working undercover."

"Sounds dangerous."

"It is." Jake made a face. "But then, just being alive in today's world is dangerous."

Considering her own present precarious situation, Sarah had to agree. "Yes, it is. Then again," she elaborated, from a position of some acquired knowledge, "living in this less-than-perfect world has always been dangerous."

"I suppose so." Jake shrugged, as if to say "that's how it goes." "Which is why this old world needs people like the Wolfe clan."

"Yes. And the next brother?" she nudged.

"That would be Royce. He's thirty-six, and a sergeant in the Pennsylvania State Police, stationed up north, near the state lines bordering Pennsylvania, New York and New Jersey. That brings us to number one son, my brother Cameron." He paused, his expression mirroring open admiration. "Cameron was and is the shining example the rest of us strive to emulate. While I was growing up, I adored him." He smiled derisively. "And, in my rebellious years, I resented him, simply because he made me adore him." He laughed. "Boy, a shrink would probably have a field day with that one."

"Not necessarily," Sarah observed. "I think it makes perfect sense. It's easy to resent someone you greatly admire, but feel you can never equal." Her smile was gentle with understanding. "Easy, and probably quite normal."

"Glad to hear it." Jake grinned at her. "So scratch the shrink."

"And what form of law enforcement is the estimable Cameron in?" she asked, bringing him back to the subject.

"He's a federal government special agent—a sort of troubleshooter, I gather. He doesn't discuss it." Jake gave a short laugh. "Hell, he doesn't talk about much of anything. The word on the street is that Cameron is referred to, by both friend and foe, as the Lone Wolfe."

"A hero type?" Sarah raised her eyebrows.

"From the top of his golden-haired head to the soles of his size twelves," Jake replied, dead serious. "He's the type of man you trust immediately and explicitly. No questions asked. If Cameron says he'll do it—*any* it—you can go to bed and sleep tight in the assurance that he will not only do it, but do it with style."

"Impressive."

"Yeah." Jake grinned. "Daunting, too."

"But necessary, in a historical sense," Sarah said, in the instructive tone she used in the lecture hall.

Jake frowned. "How so?"

"The hero type appears throughout history," she explained. "Heroes are the stuff of legend and myth.

Where would civilization be without them? They define the ideal.'' She smiled. ''The shining example you mentioned.''

''The ideal,'' Jake mused. ''Yeah, that's Cameron, and, to a somewhat lesser degree, Eric and Royce, as well.''

''But not you?''

''The ideal? The shining example?'' Jake roared with laughter. ''Not hardly, honey. I'm far from hero material. Ain't nobody dubbing me the Lone Wolfe.''

''A man apart,'' Sarah mused aloud.

''Exactly,'' Jake said. ''Apart, detached, taking care of business, while directing all our lives from a distance.'' He chuckled. ''At least he tries to direct. The rest of us give him his share of grief. At any rate, I know I do.''

''And how do your parents feel about him usurping their roles of authority?''

''Usurping? Are you kidding?'' Jake laughed. ''My mother and father set the example for the rest of us to follow in deferring to Cameron. I sometimes think my mother believes he can walk on water. And up until his death, my father began every other sentence with 'Cameron said.' ''

''Your father's gone?''

''Yes.'' Jake sighed. ''He was killed in the line of duty, almost two years ago.''

''I'm sorry,'' she murmured, meaning it.

''So am I.'' His smile was bittersweet with self-knowledge. ''His death was the catalyst that brought me home, made me reevaluate my life-style and priorities."

"And ended your rebellion?" she probed, softly.

"In spades," he confessed. "Suddenly it was grow-up time. It was time to put the toys away and get the rump in gear. I attended the police academy, then joined the force." His smile was devil-inspired. "And here I am, the model of conservative conformity you see before you."

"Uh-huh," Sarah said. I'll bet, she thought, reacting with an inner quiver to the unholy gleam in his eyes. In sheer defense against his attraction, she glanced away, and caught sight of the position of the hands on her watch. "My heavens!" she exclaimed in shocked surprise. "It's nearly midnight!"

"It happens every night at this time," Jake drawled, grimacing as he took a sip from his cup. "More importantly, the coffee's cold. How about a refill?"

"No, thank you." Sarah shook her head. "I have to get home. And don't you have to work early tomorrow?"

"No." That one small word held a wealth of satisfaction. "Tomorrow's my Saturday off." He arched his brows. "You want to do something . . . like dinner, a movie, or both?"

Sarah was tempted, sorely tempted. But memory slammed back, reminding her of the uncertainty of her position regarding Andrew Hollings and the other two students. For the past few hours, she had forgotten, relaxed her guard, enjoyed the time spent with

Jake...in truth, even those hot and heavy moments...in real truth, maybe those moments most of all.

But, she reminded herself, they were all moments out of time, lovely moments, carefree moments, free of worry and stress, hidden away here in the privacy of Jake's apartment. But to go out in public with him...

"I, er, can't recall offhand if I have anything on for tomorrow night," she lied, putting him off. "Can you give me a call tomorrow?"

"Sure." Jake stood and, raising his arms above his head, stretched luxuriously.

Sarah's breath caught in her throat at the sight. His chest expanded, muscles rippling smoothly beneath his supple skin. Lord, he was one beautiful male animal. The aching observation sent her out of her chair.

"Whenever you're ready," she said, forcing herself to walk calmly to the table near the door where she had deposited her purse when they'd arrived. "I'm a little tired."

It wasn't until later, when she was curled up in her bed, that the realization struck Sarah that she had not just felt removed from her fears during those moments out of time in Jake's apartment. With Jake, she had felt more secure, protected, safer than she had ever felt in her life.

Jake not hero material?

A sleepy smile softened Sarah's worry tightened lips. Not a hero?

She'd be the judge of that.

Jake whistled softly as he loped along the flagstone path leading to the front door of a split-level home set on a small, well-kept lot on a quiet street.

Jake felt good, better than good, as good as the weather was beautiful. The day was a picture-perfect advertisement for a brilliant Pennsylvania autumn. The copper-hued sun sailed high across the deep blue sky, driving the temperature into the mid seventies. The air was clear, mild, invigorating.

Key in hand, Jake unlocked the door and stepped inside the quiet house. "Hey, Mom, you here?"

"I'm on the phone." Maddy Wolfe stuck her head around the archway into the kitchen and smiled at him. "Come say hello to your brother."

"Which one?" Jake drawled, descending the three steps into the living room and strolling through it to the large, spotlessly clean kitchen.

"Cameron," Maddy mouthed, handing him the receiver.

"Hi, big bro," Jake said. "Where are you?"

"None of your business," the familiar, cool, in-control voice retorted.

"Aha, playing secret agent man, are you?" Jake gibed, shooting a grin at his watching mother. She frowned her disapproval; his grin widened.

"Cute, sonny boy," Cameron gibed back. "When are you going to grow up?"

Jake was neither hurt nor offended by the crack, since it was a standard comeback of his brother's. In fact, he knew he'd be hurt if Cameron should cease his serious-sounding teasing, knew he'd be afraid his brother no longer cared. "All in good time. I'm young yet, remember?" he gave his usual rejoinder. "You're the one pushing forty, old man, not me."

"Smartass," Cameron muttered, drawing a chuckle from Jake. "How's Mother?"

"You were just talking to her," he said, glancing at Maddy. "Why didn't you ask her?"

"I did, Jake," Cameron replied on a long-suffering sigh. "But you know Mother. She'd tell me she was just fine if she was literally falling apart."

Jake ran a mock-serious look over his mother's healthy-looking, still lovely face and down the length of her shapely, well-preserved sixty-year-old body. "She looks good to me, big bro," he reported. "Fit, trim and sexy as hell."

"Jake Edward Wolfe!" Maddy admonished him sharply, turning her head to hide a smile.

"Having fun, sonny?" Cameron inquired, acerbically.

"I do my best," Jake answered dryly.

"Keep up the good work, Jake." Cameron's voice was laced with quiet approval. "You know Eric, Royce and I are proud of you, don't you?"

"Yeah, bro, I know," Jake said in an emotion-thickened voice; praise from Cameron was more precious than solid gold. "You want to talk to Mom again?"

"Yes . . . and, Jake?"

"Yeah?"

"Take care."

Jake swallowed. "I will. You too."

"Of course."

The supreme confidence in Cameron's voice banished the heavy emotion and brought the grin back to Jake's lips. Turning, he held the receiver out to his mother. "The feds' fair-haired agent wants to talk to you again."

Shaking her head as if to say he was a lost cause, Maddy took the phone and murmured to Jake, "I baked your favorite cookies yesterday. They're in the cookie jar."

"Gotcha. Any coffee?"

"No." She gave him a chiding smile. "Why don't you make some while I talk to your brother?"

A half-hour later, Jake sat opposite Maddy at the kitchen table, happily dunking his favorite apple-oatmeal cookies into his coffee. When a chunk of cookie broke off and plopped into the drink, Maddy raised her eyes but got up to get him a spoon to fish it out of the cup with.

"I hope you don't do that in public," she said, settling back onto her chair.

"Mother! I am crushed!" Jake cried in feigned protest. "Must I remind you that I am a municipal representative? An officer of the law, no less?"

"Yeah, yeah . . ." Maddy said, delighting him with her youthful, teasing slang.

"Speaking of officers of the law, you hear from Eric and Royce lately?"

"Yes." Maddy's lips curved in what Jake had always thought of as her proud-mother smile. "Royce called after he went off duty late yesterday afternoon, and Eric called this morning." Her eyes contained a suspicious sparkle. "My boys watch over me like concerned hawks. Your father would be pleased."

"With the youngest, too?" Jake asked, halfway afraid of her answer.

"Ah, Jake," she murmured. "I think your father would be pleased with you, most of all."

"Because I fell in line with the family tradition?"

"No." Maddy shook her head emphatically. "Because you left home a resentful boy and returned a man."

The emotion-tight feeling invaded Jake's throat again. Hell, for all that he had scoffed at the notion during those rebellious years, family acceptance was important, after all.

"Understand," Maddy continued when he didn't respond, "I know your father would have been twice as pleased, knowing you had joined the force."

"Yeah," he agreed. "I know it, too." He hesitated, then grinned to relieve the emotional tension. "And you know what? I like being a cop."

"I'd never have guessed," his mother drawled. "Which reminds me. I read in the morning paper that

Officer Wolfe investigated a reported car-stripping yesterday.''

"Yeah." Jake grimaced. "The choppers stripped the costly buggy clean, so don't go forgetting to keep the garage locked at all times.''

"Really, Jake." She gave him a stern look. "I never forget to lock the garage—or anything else."

"Okay, okay," Jake said, laughing and holding his hands aloft in surrender. "Just a friendly reminder, is all."

"Hmm . . ." Maddy got up to clear and wipe the table. "I've got the makings for stuffed peppers," she said from the sink. "You want to come for supper?"

Jake loved stuffed peppers. Of course, Maddy knew he loved stuffed peppers. Jake suspected his mother feared he wasn't eating properly. "Can I let you know later?" he asked. "I might have a date for dinner."

"Might?" Maddy raised her eyebrows.

"I'm not sure yet," he explained. "I have to call her."

"Her?" Her eyebrows inched higher.

"A woman I met the other day," Jake explained. "Name's Sarah Cummings. She's a new associate professor of history over at Sprucewood College."

"Bright, is she?"

Her question sparked a memory flash; Jake could hear Sarah, so briefly, yet so succinctly, defining for him the role and purpose of the hero. "Oh, yeah," he answered in a decisive tone. "She's bright."

"Pretty?"

Jake could feel his features relaxing into soft, tender lines, revealing his thoughts and feelings to his astute mother. He didn't care; it wouldn't matter if he did. There was nothing he could do about it.

"Yes." Then he shrugged and shook his head. "No, she's not pretty. She's beautiful."

Maddy stared at him in open speculation for several long seconds. Then she gave a single sharp nod of her head. "Uh-huh. Like that, is it?"

"Like that?" Jake repeated. "Like what?"

"It appears to me like love at first sight," she observed seriously.

"Love at first sight!" Jake yelped. "Ah, c'mon, Mom. I just met the woman. Love at first sight." He snorted. "I think you've been watching too many television soaps."

Maddy favored him with her all-knowing-mother look. "I never watch the soaps, and you know it," she said haughtily. "But I've been around a spell, and I recognize the symptoms. You, my boy, appear to have every one of them."

"Showing symptoms does not necessarily confirm the disease," Jake retorted. "And you know that, as well."

"We'll see," she said serenely, her lips twitching. "So, are you going to call her, or what?"

Tickled once again by her use of common terminology, Jake's lips mirrored the twitch in hers. "Yes, I'm going to call her," he said in a tone of exaggerated exasperation, feeling his gut muscles clench in anticipation and excitement. "But I'm certainly not going to make the call with my mother hovering, all dewy-eyed and breathless, at my shoulder."

"Well, excuse me." Maddy sniffed disdainfully. "Go ahead," she ordered, indicating the wall phone with a flick of her hand. "Don't let me bother you. I'll go watch the Saturday-morning cartoons on the tube." She started for the living room, but paused in the archway to glance back at him, her eyes bright with the devilish, teasing light he had inherited from her. "Good luck, Jake. I'll keep my fingers crossed for you."

Thanking the universe at large for the blessing of having been born into the Wolfe family, Jake blew a kiss to his mother and reached for the phone.

Six

The telephone rang at ten forty-five.

An intense thrill shot up Sarah's spine, instantly instilling within her a memory essence of Jake. She could see him, feel him, taste him. The image warmed and chilled her at the same time; her breath became reedy, her breasts ached, her lips burned.

Jake.

Sarah froze in position, on her hands and knees, on the kitchen floor. Half the floor covering sparkled with a just-washed cleanliness. The other half was dull and dry.

The kitchen phone was mounted on the wall on the wet side of the room.

Gloved palms flat on the floor, Sarah raised her head to stare at the white phone. Her teeth sank into her lower lip; her plastic-encased fingers flexed around the cleaning rag beneath her right hand.

The phone trilled a second summons.

She had been expecting the call, dreading it, anticipating it, all morning.

What to do? she asked herself, digging her teeth deeper into her lower lip. Answer it? Ignore it? Tear the persistent instrument from the wall?

Rebellion flared to life inside Sarah. Damn fate and circumstances. She wanted to see him, be with him, get lost inside the wonder of his laughter, his embrace, his touch, his hungry mouth.

Jake.

The phone rang a third time.

Maybe it wasn't even Jake. It could be anyone, Sarah reasoned . . . a colleague, her mother, a disembodied someone selling replacement windows, an official from a magazine distribution company, calling to inform her happily that she had won the sweepstakes grand prize of a zillion dollars.

Yeah, right.

The phone pealed for the fourth time.

Sarah gnawed on the abused lip.

Fool, she upbraided herself, dismissing the twinges of strain streaking up her arms from the pressure on her flattened palms. Why hadn't she followed her first inclination this morning and bypassed the paper to get an early start on the weekly cleaning chore? Sarah asked herself, pushing her body upright. If she had left the news for later, she wouldn't have read the account that had set her mental wheels spinning in speculation and supposition.

The fifth ring shrilled.

Sarah made a low, moaning sound deep in her throat. She hated having a phone ring on and on unanswered at any time, but she hated it even more now, when she felt certain the caller was Jake. She took one step, then hesitated, her right foot raised slightly, teetering on the edge of indecision.

If only she hadn't read that article in the paper. Her foot came down, in place. But, of course, after Jake's name jumped off the page at her, it had been impossible for her not to read it.

The phone rang for the seventh time.

Sarah shivered. Damn it! Why, why, why, had she immediately felt, sensed, a connection between Andrew Hollings and his friends and the account of a local resident's car being stripped? She had nothing to base such a suspicion upon, and yet . . . and yet, Sarah knew, inside, that there had to be a connection between the theft and the students' odd behavior.

The eighth trill beat against her eardrums.

Jake.

The intense desire to hear his voice simmered to a roiling boil inside Sarah, stirring up doubts and denials.

Pure speculation, she told herself, taking another two steps toward the phone. In truth, she knew nothing. She was spooked, that was all, spooked into drawing conclusions from sheer speculation and supposition.

The ninth ring seared her nervous system like an electric shock.

Sarah longed to dismiss her speculative notions and run to the phone. She had reached the point of yearning to hear Jake's voice at the other end of the line. She desperately wanted to accept his invitation for dinner and a movie, and yes, anything else he might suggest. Damn it, she wanted so badly to see him, be with him... touch him... in every way. Her body felt like an empty vessel, needing the strength and fullness of his to make her complete. It made no difference whether she had known him two days or two hundred years. She wanted Jake. It was as basic and honest as that. She took the three necessary steps to the phone and raised her hand.

But what if her instinctive reaction to that article was correct? Sarah asked herself, letting her hand hover over the receiver. Suppose her suppositions had validity. The article had said the police theorized that the theft had occurred sometime in the predawn hours yesterday morning. She had seen Andrew and his friends not many hours later, had noted their furtive nervousness. But, more importantly, she had heard the sibilant, whispery tenor of Andrew's voice, reiterating his innocent-sounding advice.

Silence is golden, Miss Cummings.

A chill of dread shuddered through Sarah.

The phone rang for the tenth time.

Coincidence? Sarah wanted to believe it, needed to believe it. She just couldn't. Call it intuition, gut instinct, whatever, but she just *knew*. Somehow, in some way, Andrew and his friends had been involved in stripping that car. And if her screaming intuition was right, she could not afford to be seen in public in the company of the police officer who had investigated the reported theft.

Sarah didn't become aware of holding her breath until the realization registered that the phone was not going to jangle an eleventh command.

The sudden silence felt as if the earth and every living thing on it had stopped breathing.

Silence is golden, Miss Cummings.

Golden? Sarah challenged the memory echo. No, silence was not golden, it was brass, and it carried the bitter, coppery taste of fear and despair.

"Jake." Whispering his name, Sarah lowered her forehead to the receiver.

Sheer determination and concentrated physical activity got Sarah through the rest of the morning and into midafternoon. The apartment had probably never received such a thorough cleaning. Even the windows sparkled in the autumn sunlight.

Throughout the intervening hours, Sarah had engaged in a running dialogue with herself, dissecting the situation. On one hand, she argued against the probability of Andrew and his friends being involved in anything illegal. Why would they be? she asked herself. She had made a point of checking their school records. All three young men came from well-off families; they wanted for nothing financially. Why, then, for what earthly reason, would any one of the three even dream of committing an act of thievery?

It didn't make sense.

Sarah conceded the point, then turned to examining the question from another perspective—her own. She had heard the snatches of conversation between them, and although they were suspicious in content, they were not conclusive proof of guilt, not by a long shot. Except for the added factor of Andrew's muttered warning to her.

The threatening sound of his voice, along with the frightening intensity of his narrow-eyed stare, clinched the matter for Sarah. They were up to no good, and she knew it.

So then, where did that leave the associate professor? Sarah asked herself, wielding the vacuum cleaner for all she was worth. Right behind the eight ball, she answered herself, shoving a chair to one side.

Naturally, during the course of her cleaning frenzy, Sarah did consider options other than remaining silent. She could present her suspicions to the police, or the college dean, or even ask the advice of the head of her own department. Of course she could, she derided herself. And afterward she could slink away with the sound of their collective laughter ringing inside her head.

Proof. Proof. Proof. A necessary factor, proof, if one set about pointing the finger of blame. And the bottom line was inescapable: she had no concrete proof.

Giving the bedroom windows what for, Sarah industriously applied the cloth to the pane...and her mind to her personal dilemma.

Another bottom line. Sarah wanted to spend time with Jake, a lot of time. She liked him, more than liked him. And, even with the crackling physical attraction that sizzled between them, she felt comfortable with him, as one would feel with an old friend, rather than a person one had so recently met—which, to her way of thinking, was somewhat amazing in itself. Just by being himself, Jake amused her, delighted her, excited her.

Had it really only been two days since they met?

Incredible. But there it was, plain as that streak down the center of the window. The streak posed no problem; one careful swipe of the cloth and it was gone. Sarah's feelings for Jake were not as easily dealt with.

Jake was a cop, and therefore a potential threat to Andrew and his friends.

And Sarah was getting pretty tired of bottom lines. The bedroom windows finished, she headed grimly into the living room to attack the two windows there.

Perhaps she was just being silly, or perhaps she was the biggest coward going, but to Sarah's way of thinking, there was simply no getting around it—by continuing to see Jake, and be seen with him, she would be placing herself in jeopardy... herself, and possibly Jake, as well.

Jake didn't have a clue about her suspicions, and so he'd be vulnerable, exposed to unforeseen danger.

Sarah's hand stilled on the windowpane. Would they hurt Jake, strike against him when he was unaware, unprepared? The thought sent a spear of panic skittering through her. They? she shook her head. Maybe not them, collectively—but Andrew? Sarah had a combined mental image and echo of Andrew as he had looked, sounded, while issuing his warning to her. Conviction settled on her like a heavy burden.

Andrew would not hesitate in implementing any measure he deemed necessary to protect himself.

Shoulders drooping, Sarah stepped back from the partially cleaned window. Despite her personal opinion regarding Jake as a hero, there was no way she could knowingly place him in the position of sitting duck.

When Jake called, if he called, she had no choice but to tell him she could not see him... not tonight, and not in the foreseeable future.

The phone rang at exactly 3:26. Sarah knew the time because she had been glancing at the clock every ten or twelve seconds since around two. Squaring her shoulders, she lifted the receiver on the second ring.

"Hello?"

"Hi." Jake's voice, soft and sensuous, flowed through the line like warm honey. "How are you?"

"I'm fine," she lied. I'm miserable, she said in despairing silence. "And you?"

"Anxious."

She knew. Of course she knew. Still, she had to ask, "Anxious about what?"

"Sa-rah, hon-ey..." He drew her name, and the endearment, out, like a long, slow caress. "You know darn well that I'm anxious about hearing your answer."

Sarah inhaled, determined to say no.

"Will you come out with me tonight?" he asked, in that same honeyed, coaxing voice.

"Yes." Sarah's hand flew up to cover her traitorous mouth. So much for determination.

"Thank you." Jake's soft tone contained a wealth of relief. "I promise you won't regret it."

Sarah stifled a sigh; she already regretted it. The warm honey of his voice must have flowed into her ear and directly to her brain, smothering it. "Did you have anything in particular in mind?" A loaded question if she had ever heard one, Sarah upbraided herself. His low laughter confirmed her opinion, but, to his credit, Jake didn't stoop to sexual innuendo.

"What do you think of the idea of running into Philly for dinner and a show?"

Sarah brightened at his suggestion; if they skipped out of town, it would lessen their chances of being seen together by any of the three students.

"A show?" she repeated. "Do you mean a movie?"

"No, a Broadway show." Jake went on to mention a road-company group currently doing a run at a center-city theater of a smash musical that was still playing to near-capacity audiences in New York City.

"Oh, I'd love to see that show," Sarah said, with unbridled enthusiasm. "I've heard it's wonderful, but isn't it too late to get tickets for tonight?"

"I've got them," he reported, a note of satisfaction in his voice. "I called the theater and got the last two seats available. They're in the nosebleed section of the balcony," he warned her, "but the guy in the ticket office assured me the location of the seats affords an unobstructed view." He chuckled. "And we can take my binoculars."

"I can bring my opera glasses," Sarah offered eagerly, feeling giddy with relief and anticipation.

"There you go—we're set," Jake said, laughing.

"What time, Jake?" she asked, slanting a quick look at the wall clock.

"That depends on whether you prefer to have dinner before or after the show," Jake replied. "I know of several restaurants close by to the theater. You tell me your preference, and I'll call and make reservations."

"It doesn't matter to me," Sarah assured him, falling back on the traditional female response. "Which one would you prefer, before or after?"

Fortunately, Jake appeared unwilling to engage in that traditional man-woman stalemate. "Both," he replied at once.

"Both?" Sarah blinked. "I don't understand."

"Simple. The solution, that is, not you." Jake laughed. "We can have an early dinner before the show, and a snack after the show. How does that sound?"

"As wonderful *as* the show," Sarah admitted, joining in on his laughter. "So, what time, Jake?"

"Well, the curtain's at eight, and we don't want to rush through dinner," he mused aloud. "So suppose I make the reservations for six?" He didn't wait for a response from her, but continued on in the same musing tone, "Considering the Saturday-evening traffic, I'd suggest we leave a little after five. That'll give us ample time to park the car and walk to the restaurant. Okay?"

"Okay, I'll be ready," she said, not even bothering to conceal the eagerness bubbling over in her voice.

Sarah glanced at the clock again as she replaced the receiver. It was 3:40. Yikes! she thought, spinning around and dashing for the bathroom. That gave her only an hour and a half to get ready. She had to take a shower, shampoo her hair, do her nails and find something to wear.

The something to wear that she finally decided would have to do was another sand-washed silk confection in blending shades of green and brown. It was a filmy two-piece ensemble consisting of a blouse with a scooped neckline and sleeves tapering to loose, cuffed sleeves, and a full skirt that swirled enticingly around her ankles.

With sure and practiced fingers, Sarah piled her thick hair into a loose knot at the back of her head, allowing strategically placed tendrils to escape at her temples and nape. Her sole adornments were a pair of large gold hoop earrings.

Since her color was already heightened by excitement, Sarah merely enhanced the glow with a quick pat of translucent foundation, a brush of earth-tone blusher, a swish of muted olive eye shadow and a glide of terra-cotta lipstick. She was waving her hands in the air, drying the second application of polish on her nails—a vibrant golden-bronze shade that matched her sling-backed heels and evening bag—when the doorbell rang at precisely ten after five.

If Sarah had thought that Jake looked terrific dressed in a navy blue Windbreaker and a blue-and-white striped shirt—and she had—the impact he made on her senses when she opened the door for him carried double the breath-stealing effect.

Attired for an evening out in a charcoal brown suit, a pale yellow silk shirt and a yellow, brown and gold patterned silk tie, Jake looked like he had just finished filming a television commercial for a new, sexy cologne for the "in" man.

His freshly washed toast-colored hair glinted with golden highlights. The burnished skin stretched tautly over his strong features gleamed from a recent shave. His deep blue eyes sparkled with expectation.

"Hi." His low voice had acquired another coat of honeyed enticement. The soft, delectable sound of it went to her head like potent wine.

"Hi." Sarah stared at him in unabashed admiration, fighting to maintain a semblance of normalcy while trying to breathe, think, act, like a rational person.

"You're beautiful," Jake murmured, devouring her with a slow, encompassing look, the blue of his eyes darkening with flaring passion.

"Th—thank you..." Sarah could barely speak; she couldn't think at all, which freed her tongue to blurt out the truth. "You're beautiful, too."

Jake's burst of delighted laughter rumbled through the narrow apartment hallway. "Men aren't beautiful," he told her teasingly when his laughter had dwindled to a smile.

"You are," Sarah maintained, repaying his complimentary appraisal by running an assessing glance over his tall, angular, tightly knit body. "Handsome, too."

The glow of humor fled from his fantastic eyes, replaced by a leaping flame so hot in appearance that it seared Sarah to the depths of her being. "Be careful, honey," he advised her in a raspy whisper. "I've just discovered that I'm susceptible to flattery from you. Much more of it, and we might find ourselves right here, making a meal of each other and putting on a showstopping performance of our own."

The realization that his warning held infinite appeal jolted Sarah into awareness of where they were. Good grief! Jake was standing in the hallway, and she was hanging on to the doorknob as if it were a lifeline!

"Ah...well, in that case..." Sarah rushed on, painfully aware that she was babbling, "I think we'd better go."

"Coward." Jake's smile taunted her, and the lights dancing in his eyes excited her.

Releasing her death grip on the doorknob, Sarah silently endorsed his opinion, gulping as she spun away to grab the soft caramel-colored soft wool cape and bronze bag she had tossed on the chair just inside the door.

"I'm ready," she announced, swinging the cape about her shoulders before he had a chance to step forward to assist her and send her excitement level soaring with his feather-light touch, as he had last evening.

Jake didn't say anything; he didn't have to say a word. His laughing eyes said volumes about the amusement she afforded him with her show of skittishness and trepidation.

The atmosphere inside the car was charged with sexual tension. Sarah imagined she could feel the shimmering electricity skipping over her sensitized nerves and her responsively quivering flesh.

Her trembling fingers fumbled with the simple process of inserting the prong of the safety belt into the buckle. Muttering a curse of frustration and self-disgust, she made another stab with the prong—and missed again. A shudder of intense awareness shot through her at the touch of Jake's warm flesh as he brushed her hands away to attach the belt for her.

"I know how you feel," he murmured, staring deeply into her widened eyes, while setting off tiny explosions deep inside her with the brief contact of the back of his long fingers against the contracting muscles of her lower abdomen. "I feel like I just might fly off in seventeen directions, too."

"You . . . you do?" Sarah asked, in a parched little voice, staring at him in helpless wonder.

"Of course." A wry smile slanted his tempting mouth. "As I told you last night, I want you, and since last night the wanting has grown even—" his smile curved derisively "—harder than before."

Words of protest, shock, denial, jumped from Sarah's mind to her tongue. Lies, all lies. She refused the words passage from her dry lips. One small word escaped her guard, the word she had repeated in silence, like a litany, throughout the day.

"Jake."

His eyes flickered. He shuddered, moved closer, then pulled back, shaking his head. A taut silence held sway for a moment. He broke it with a sound that was half laugh, half sigh.

"What is it with this car?" Jake mused aloud, slanting a twinkling sidelong look at her. "I'm beginning to suspect that the last time I had it washed, one of the attendants gave it a shot of deodorant spray bought from a company called Aphrodisiacs R Us.''

His droll observation achieved its intended purpose. Sarah burst out laughing, relieving the strain and tension humming between them.

''Will you get this car moving?'' she ordered, swallowing another rising tide of mirth. ''I didn't take time for lunch, and I'm hungry.'' Narrowing her eyes in warning, she quickly added, ''And don't you dare do a double entendre on that last word. Just let it remain the last word.''

''Would I do that?'' Jake murmured, more to himself than to her. His lips twitched. ''Probably,'' he admitted, flipping the ignition switch to fire the engine. ''So then it's a good thing she warned me against doing that,'' he went on, still talking to himself, as he eased the car away from the curb and into the late-Saturday afternoon traffic. ''Keeps me on my best behavior... I guess.''

''And it's my guess that your wrappings are getting a mite frayed around the edges,'' Sarah observed, relaxing with a sigh against the cradling seat back.

Jake kept up a nonsensical running commentary throughout the drive into the city, and by the time he pulled the car into the parking garage they were laughing easily together, like two teenagers out on a lark.

The restaurant Jake had chosen was really a pub, with an Irish ambience and a hail-fellow-well-met atmosphere. The hostess was pretty and friendly, chattering away as if they were old and valued friends as she led them to a high-backed corner booth that afforded conversational privacy. The indirect lighting was diffuse, dim, the primary glow stemming from amber bulbs fixed near to the ceiling. The amber-globed oil lamps placed on each table gave little additional illumination.

The menus the hostess gave them turned out to offer another source of amusement for Jake, simply because Sarah had to dig her glasses out of her bag to read it.

"What's so funny?" she asked, frowning as she squinted at the selections, which were printed in a small typeface.

"Nothing," Jake said, continuing to grin at her. "It's just, well, the day I first noticed you sitting in that back booth at Dave's place, I thought you resembled an owl in those big round glasses." He held up a hand when she opened her mouth to protest. "A very attractive and interesting-looking owl," he said cajolingly. Then he ruined the effect by adding, "But an owl just the same."

Though Sarah gave him a fierce frown, she couldn't suppress the laughter bubbling up in her throat.

The food was delicious, accompanied by mutual teasing and bouts of laughter from Jake and Sarah. They lingered over the wine. Jake had allowed himself just one glass.

"I'm driving," he said. "But you may have as many as you like."

Recalling how quickly the wine had gone to her head just last night, Sarah, too, declined a second drink.

Nursing the excellent dry white, they lost track of the time, and they might have missed the curtain for the show if the hostess hadn't stopped by their booth to give them a gentle reminder.

The show turned out to be every bit as wonderful as Sarah had heard it was, and they left the theater humming snatches of one of the catchy musical numbers.

The tiring effects of Sarah's hell-bent industriousness in her cleaning frenzy earlier in the day caught up with her while she and Jake were having a snack in the same pub where they had eaten dinner. Even the coffee she had was unequal to the need for sleep that was weighing down her eyelids.

"Tired?" Jake asked, after her third smothered yawn.

"Yes," Sarah admitted with a rueful smile; she really hated to see the evening end. "I'm sorry, but I was up early and cleaning the apartment most of the day, and I can hardly keep my eyes open."

"Nothing to be sorry for," Jake said, motioning to the waiter for their check. "But now I'm confused about something."

"Confused?" Sarah frowned. "About what?"

"You did say you were up early?"

"Yes." Sarah felt so sleepy, she actually didn't get the drift of where he was heading. "So?"

Jake shrugged. "I called, in the morning. I thought that maybe you'd gone shopping or something."

"Oh." Sarah felt like a fool . . . a deceitful fool. "Yes, I mean, no, I didn't go out. I must have been cleaning the bathroom, running the water, and didn't hear the phone."

"Probably." Jake accepted her excuse without question, making her feel even more deceptive.

"Sorry," Sarah murmured, meaning it.

"No matter. We're together." Jake's smile chased the guilt from her mind, if not the sleepiness; she yawned again. "Come along, sleepyhead," he urged, polishing off his second cup of coffee in one gulp before sliding from the bench seat. "Time to head for home."

With her head settled against the seat's headrest, Sarah had slipped into a doze before they were out of the city. Not quite asleep, yet not fully awake, she floated on a lovely cloud, dreamy and secure with Jake at the wheel beside her. In her misty dream, she and Jake danced to the haunting strains of the love ballad from the show.

When they arrived at Sarah's apartment, Jake helped her from the car and steered her up the steps and to her door.

"Oh, Jake," Sarah whispered, rummaging in her bag for her key. "I had a lovely time. Thank you."

"Thank you," he whispered in return. "I had a lovely time, too."

The door swung open; Sarah stood still, captured by the expression in Jake's dark blue eyes. A thrill shot through her as he took a step, closing the distance between them. Suddenly she was wide-awake, alert, all her senses alive and aware.

"Can we make it even more lovely with a good-night kiss, honey?" His voice was low, enticing.

Sarah knew, with irrevocable certainty, that if she allowed the kiss, it wouldn't end there. She knew, and yet she didn't hesitate. Instantly she made a conscious decision to spend the night with Jake . . . in her bed.

"Yes," she answered, moving away from him to step into her living room. "But not out in the hall." Reaching out, she grasped his hand and gave it a light tug. "Come in, Jake."

Seven

Jake's eyes flickered in surprise, but he didn't hesitate. Without uttering a word, he crossed the threshold, shut and locked the door and, turning, drew her very gently, very carefully to him.

"You're sure, honey?" he asked, in a dry, not-quite-steady murmur. His gaze delved into hers, a laser-blue light seeking the truth.

"Yes, Jake." Sarah slid her tongue over her excitement-dried lips, and shivered as his glittering gaze fastened onto her mouth. "I'm sure."

His hands moved across her shoulders to her cape, then under it. The soft wool garment slid unnoticed to the floor. His suit jacket followed a moment later.

Sarah didn't move. She couldn't. All she could do was watch as, slowly, maddeningly, Jake lowered his head. Quivering in anticipation, Sarah parted her lips. His mouth touched hers in a feather-light caress.

"Sarah," Jake groaned into her mouth. The sound of her name echoed inside her spinning head.

"Kiss me." Sarah heard the raw, pleading note in her voice. She didn't care; it didn't matter. All that mattered in the world, her world, was his mouth.

He answered her plea. Slanting his head, Jake touched her lips with his, and made them his own. They were chaste, sweet, and for an infinitely long, frustrating moment he maintained a light, delicate touch.

The very delicacy of his kiss was an inducement to madness and abandon. Moaning a protest low in her throat, Sarah raised her hands to grasp his head, urging him, his mouth, into fuller contact with hers.

Obeying her silent command, Jake took her mouth in a kiss so fiery that she felt the scorching brand in the depths of her femininity. His tongue caressed, tormented, the tender inner skin of her lower lip, making her frantic for more of him, and still more. Growing desperate, Sarah plied her own tongue, luring him inside.

A low grunt of satisfaction rumbled in Jake's throat, and then he plunged in, his tongue filling the moist cavern of her mouth, igniting a singeing spark in her body that had her clinging to him, her curling fingers anchoring in the crisp strands of his thick hair.

It was like coming home.

The vague thought flitted through Sarah's mind as she settled into his crushing embrace, conforming the round softness of her body to the angular hardness of his.

And Jake's body was hard, from his plundering lips to the solid width of his shoulders and chest to the taut muscles of his thighs, and every inch in between. His hands pressed against her spine, urging her closer and closer still, until Sarah felt fused to him, mouth to mouth, breasts to chest, hipbone to hipbone, womanhood to manhood.

Raking the sweetness of her mouth with his tongue, Jake curved his body over hers, bowing her spine, arching her up, into him, his heat, his hardness.

Sarah's world, narrowed down to the small space their fused bodies occupied, burst into flame. It was a beautiful blaze, breathtaking, exhilarating, life-giving.

Like the fabled phoenix rising from the ashes, Sarah's spirit soared on the wings of a consuming passion unlike anything she had ever before experienced.

She burned, outside, inside, to be one with Jake, to be filled by Jake, to belong to Jake.

Conveying her desire, her burning need, Sarah scored his scalp with her fingernails and moved her body sinuously against his aroused flesh.

Jake growled and pulled his mouth from hers to blaze a fiery trail of stinging kisses and gentle bites down the arched column of her neck. His tongue unerringly found the erratically beating pulse at the base of her throat, and teased it into a thundering that thrummed against her eardrums.

Murmuring his name, Sarah glided her lips along the curved edge of his ear and dipped the tip of her tongue into the small hollow. His body jerked at her delicate touch, thrusting his pelvis forward. Sarah felt the expanding strength of his need, and gloried in it.

She skimmed her palms over his shoulders, down his arched back, to clasp him by the hips, pulling him, his hardness, more tightly to her yielding softness.

"Sarah, Sarah, Sarah..." As he murmured her name, Jake lowered his hands to grasp her waist, and as if his legs would no longer support him, he dropped to his knees on the floor in front of her and buried his face in the silky material pooling in the valley between her breasts.

Sarah went weak, her knees threatening to buckle, toppling her to the floor before him. Clutching his shoulders, she remained upright, shuddering in response to the sensations streaking through her body at the wet, hungry touch of his lips closing around the tip of one breast.

It was heaven. It was hell. It was beautiful. It was unbearable. It was too much. It was not enough.

Not nearly enough.

Sarah wanted, wanted, wanted. The wanting enveloped her mind, driving out conscious thought and reason.

"Jake." Her voice had been reduced to a mere whisper, barely a sound at all, a sighing murmur screaming to him of her need, her desire, her unleashed passion.

As nearly nonexistent as it was, Jake heard her cry, and the supplication entwined with it. He drew his head back, leaving the hard tip of her breast pushing against the moist spot on the silky material. Raising his head, he again stared with probing intent into her eyes. A moment, two, and then he tightened his grasp on her waist and pulled her to him to slowly drag her body down the length of his.

Sarah felt the carpet fibers scrape her knees, and then her body being lowered to the floor. Jake followed her down, flattening her breasts with his chest, crushing her lips beneath his greedy mouth.

At least the carpet's clean.

The irrelevant consideration zinged through her mind, to her sense of humor and out her throat on a breathless gurgle of laughter.

Jake pulled back to gaze at her, a puzzled frown scoring his brow. "Something's funny?"

Sarah bit her lip and shook her head, creating a crackling static with the friction of her hair against the carpet. "I...I just had a dumb thought," she explained.

He looked skeptical. "What dumb thought?"

The sudden release of the sensual tension of the previous minutes took its toll in a bout of the giggles. "I...I just thought that—" Sarah paused to draw a controlling breath "—at least the carpet's clean."

Looking stunned, Jake stared at her 〔 stopping seconds. Then a twitch tilted up the of his compressed lips, and his shoulders be〔 〔o shake. "You sure do know how to bring a man down to earth," he told her accusingly, nearly choking on the laughter he was obviously suppressing. His smile took a crooked turn. "And to his knees," he muttered wryly.

"Oh, Jake, I'm sorry." Contrite, Sarah stroked her fingers down his smooth cheek to the muscle kicking along his squared jaw. "I didn't mean to spoil the moment."

Now his smile curved at a sensuous angle. "Spoiled?" He dipped his head to administer a quick, hard kiss to her ruefully set mouth, and gave a low grunt of satisfaction when she shivered in response. "Nothing's spoiled, honey." His smile grew wickedly daring. "Or even deflated, for that matter." He rotated his hips against her to prove his assertion.

Gasping at the sensations his movement sent rioting through her, Sarah arched her spine reflexively and tightened her grip on his shoulders. Her senses swam, drowning once more in a molten flow of sensuality. Straining up, she sought his smiling mouth with her tingling lips.

"More?" he murmured, teasing her with tiny hit-and-run touches of his lips against hers.

"Yes, yes," Sarah pleaded, digging her nails into the silky material covering his shoulders. "And I don't care if the carpet's clean or filthy."

"But I do." Jake drew back. "Not about the carpet," he continued, moving into a kneeling position next to her. "I care about you." He slid one arm under her shoulders, the other under her knees.

Anticipating his intent, Sarah held her breath and curled her arms tightly around his neck.

"I lost my head for a moment there," he confessed. Taking a deep breath, he lifted her up, close to his chest, and surged to his feet. When he was standing, he remained still for a moment, his chest heaving from the exertion.

Her senses stabilizing, Sarah eased the pent-up breath from her emotion-tightened throat and gazed up at him in enthralled silence.

"I'm damn near exploding with wanting you, honey, but not like that, rolling around on a hard floor." His blue eyes darkened to the deepest sapphire. "Oh, no, not like that," he whispered, bending his head to brush his mouth over her parted lips. "I want to savor each and every nuance along the way from excitement to explosion."

"Oh, Jake." She sighed and pressed her lips to the side of his throat. "So do I."

Her admission set him moving, through the living room and into the bedroom. Clinging to him, Sarah closed her eyes, deciding she rather enjoyed the sensation of being literally swept off her feet by her hero, rendered breathless and eager, like a heroine straight out of history or a movie or a romance novel.

And Jake *was* a hero, she mused dreamily, sighing as he set her upright next to the bed. Her hero... whether he saw himself in the role or not. A secret smile curving her lips, Sarah raised her head and parted her lips in excited expectation of his kiss.

Jake didn't disappoint her. Murmuring her name, he fitted his mouth to hers, instantly submerging her once more in a sensuous realm of glittering sensations.

Sarah responded without hesitation. Her defenses were not only down, they were utterly demolished. It had been so very long since she had felt the passionate demands of the flesh, and even then the demands had been as weak as water in comparison to the wine-heady clamor she experienced each time Jake kissed her, touched her, as he was at this moment.

His hands stroked her shoulders, her arms, her back, bringing her flesh to glorious life with each successive caress. Sarah reciprocated in turn, gliding her palms from the back of his neck to his shoulders and down his chest. In a well-choreographed dance of love, they moved in unison, her fingers working on the buttons of his shirt as his hands tugged her blouse from the waistband of her skirt.

There was no fumbling, no groping. Between heated, ever-deepening kisses and warm, soft murmurs, they removed the material barriers of convention between their two separate beings, which were raging to blend into one.

When at last the final wisps of cloth were tossed aside, they sank onto the bed as one. Eager hands reached to touch, to know, trembling fingers explored quivering flesh.

Jake drew the tips of his fingers along the curve of her breast. "So soft, so beautiful."

"You taste salty," Sarah murmured, gliding the tip of her tongue along the curve of his shoulder.

He gave a shuddering response, then drew one from her by gently lashing the crest of her breast with his tongue. Gasping, she arched her back, and carefully sank her teeth into his supple skin in a delicate love bite.

Grunting his enjoyment and appreciation of her gentle aggression, Jake drew the tight tip of her breast into his mouth. Sensations splintered inside Sarah at the pleasure inflicted by his suckling lips.

Tension spiraled, building higher and higher. Shuddering, moaning, she skimmed her hands down his torso. Sarah's palms tingled at the feel of his warm, passion-moistened skin, the muscles clenching beneath her hands.

"Yes, yes..." Jake's voice was little more than a hoarse, ragged groan. "Sarah, touch me, please..."

She hesitated a moment, but then, crying out in reaction to the pull of his lips on her breast, she slid her palms lower, over the flat tautness of his belly, and lower still, to the apex of his thighs.

Jake drew a harsh breath and went still, as if arrested by the feelings instilled by her skin gliding over his, waiting, waiting for a more intimate caress.

Quivering, barely breathing herself, Sarah reached down and cradled him with her trembling fingers.

Jake's pent-up breath whooshed from his throat, bathing her breast in warm moisture, tightening the tension inside her, emboldening her to further exploration. Marveling at his silky hardness, she curled her fingers around him.

"Sarah." His voice had been reduced to a raspy whisper. "Oh, Sarah, that feels so good." Deserting her other breast, his hand slid to her waist, to her hip, to her—

"Jake."

Sarah didn't recognize the voice that cried from her throat. Her mind spinning, her senses rioting out of control, she arched her body, high, into the pleasure-giving probe of his caressing, stroking fingers.

The tension spiral compressed, radiating shards of fiery desire into the core of her femininity. Sarah couldn't bear it, and yet she craved more.

"Jake, Jake, please," she sobbed, writhing in response to the deepening intimacy of his searing touch. Not fully aware of reciprocating his caress, she wrenched a groan from the depths of his throat with the movement of her fingers caging his smooth, heated flesh.

"Yes, now," Jake muttered, as if through teeth clenched against loss of control. Grasping her by the hips, he raised her from the bed, moved into position between her thighs, and stared down at her hands, still cradling his quivering flesh. A shudder ripped through him as she slowly withdrew her hands in a lingering caress.

"Yes, Jake!" she cried. "Now!"

"A moment," he murmured, reaching for the small square packet he had placed on the nightstand. The tremor in his fingers betrayed his heightened passion as he swiftly adjusted the sheathing protection.

"Now." He moved to the very portal, paused for a tormenting heartbeat, then thrust forward, filling the aching emptiness inside her.

The tension spiral went crazy, and Sarah went crazy with it. Clinging to him, afraid she'd fly apart if she let go, she moved in time with the ever-accelerating, hard-thrusting rhythm of his body. His mouth captured hers, his tongue reflecting the possession of his pounding body.

The tension spiral tightened, tightened, tightened, and then it snapped, shattering into a million lights, sparkling throughout Sarah's entire being, erupting from her passion-dried lips in the cry of his name into his mouth.

"Jake!"

Her muted scream seemingly lashing him on, Jake thrust deeper and deeper. Then, shudders cascading the length of his body, he tore his mouth from hers, calling her name, over and over, in a harsh, exultant cry of intense release.

* * *

A chill permeating the air brought Jake to the edge of consciousness. Not fully awake, yet no longer asleep, he felt confused by the conflicting sensations of cold and warmth, and by a deep inner sense of well-being. He lay on his left side, which was warm, but his right side, exposed to the air, felt chilled to the bone.

Had he tossed off the covers sometime during the night? he wondered, yawning. A movement beside him brought a question to his sleep-clouded mind.

Movement?

Fighting his way out of the lingering fog of slumber, Jake pried his eyes open. Memory rushed back, clear and exciting, at the sight that met his startled gaze.

The woman snuggled against him was the direct cause of his partial warmth, and his complete well-being.

Sarah.

A smile, soft and tender, curved Jake's lips, lips that could taste the distinctive flavor of Sarah. He whispered a long sigh of utter satisfaction.

Never, never, throughout all his years of wandering, or even before, with any of the girls and women he had known, had Jake felt anything even remotely akin to the shattering and glorious joy he had experienced with Sarah.

She murmured, shivered and snuggled closer, dispelling his bemusement. Sarah was obviously feeling the cold in her sleep. Chastising himself for falling asleep so soon after attaining what he believed was the nearest he would ever get to paradise, Jake reached across Sarah to grasp a corner of the coverlet and pulled it over them, cocooning them within its warmth-giving comfort.

The warmth enveloping him, Jake set about easing his cramped muscles. Sarah's head was pillowed on his left arm, and it was sending out warning signals of complaint. Moving slowly, carefully, so as not to disturb her, he slid his arm from beneath her and slid a real pillow under her head to take its place. Sarah slept on. Encouraged, Jake shifted his hips and stretched out his long legs, laying the right one over hers. Sarah was still out for the count. Fearless now, he curled his right arm around her waist and gently drew her closer to the rapidly increasing heat of his naked body. A victorious smile sashayed across his mouth at the silky feel of her skin gliding against his hair-roughened, quickening body.

He was sorely tempted to wake her.

Sarah sighed contentedly in her sleep.

Jake felt her sigh in the depths of his soul.

How was it possible, he mused, ruthlessly tamping down his passion, that this particular woman possessed the singular power to affect him so deeply, so completely?

Pondering the question, Jake drew distracting pleasure from the simple exercise of detailing her delicate features. Sarah *was* lovely, with her satiny skin, her mass of auburn hair and her soft brown eyes. But surely the strength of her attraction went deeper than facial beauty. Of course, she had a delectable body that could drive him, and probably dozens of other men, straight to distraction, if not perdition. But he had known other women equally beautiful, even more so in form, as well as facial features.

Dismissing mere good looks as a consideration, Jake delved deeper for an answer. On numerous occasions, Sarah had revealed to him a sharp intelligence, and Jake did appreciate a bright, if not necessarily savvy, woman. Also, in addition to her other attributes, she possessed a keen, often wry, sense of humor. Jake acknowledged that of all the factors in her favor, Sarah's sense of humor was very likely the most appealing and important to him.

In other words, Jake reflected, as far as he personally was concerned, Sarah had one hell of a lot going for her, more than enough to instill within him strong feelings of not only wildly elated hormones raging to merge, but of protection, tenderness, caring and...

Love at first sight?

Jake's thought process came to an abrupt halt as an echo of his mother's voice rang inside his head. Could it be possible? he wondered, staring, amazed, into Sarah's sleep-vulnerable countenance. Was it really possible to fall in love at first sight?

Jake's memory did an about-face, taking him back to his first sight of her at Dave's place. He was prepared to admit that from his first sight of Sarah, looking endearingly owlish in those big round glasses, he had been instantly attracted, instantly interested, almost as instantly aroused. But love?

Love was heavy, serious business, encompassing commitment and fidelity. The kind of stuff families were made of. Did his attraction, his interest, even his desire, run that deep?

"Jake." Sarah murmured his name in her sleep. A small, sweet smile curved her slightly parted lips.

Jake had the weird sensation of his insides turning to mush. Did his feelings run that deep? Jake mused, his own lips tilting in a smile of willing defeat.

Oh, yeah. Maybe even deeper.

Eight

Sarah woke to a tickling brush and a prodding nudge from a very sexy man. Opening her eyes a fraction, she stared into Jake's passion-darkened eyes.

"I'm sorry," he murmured, offering her a heart-stopping morning-after smile. "Go back to sleep, honey. I didn't mean to wake you."

"Well, maybe *you* didn't," she said softly, "but a rather persistent part of your anatomy did."

Jake maintained a straight face for all of ten seconds, then burst out laughing. "I knew it. I knew it was your sense of humor that got to me," he crowed, managing to thoroughly confuse and amuse her.

"Really?" Sarah opened her eyes wide and fluttered her lashes. "And here I thought it was a part of *my* anatomy that got to you."

"That, too." Jake's grin was positively wolfish. He moved his hips, eliciting a gasp from her.

"You're incorrigible," she scolded him, unsuccessfully fighting a giggle.

"Insatiable, too," he drawled, slowly, tantalizingly raising the leg he had moments before slipped between her thighs.

Sarah shivered responsively to the arousing feel of his muscle-bunched thigh pressing against her. Melting, figuratively and literally, she let her eyes close, and, reacting reflexively, she moved her lower body slowly back and forth.

Jake inhaled sharply, then lowered his head to capture her parted lips in the heated snare of his hard, hungry mouth. His tongue raked across the edges of her teeth, then speared into the honeyed recess of her mouth.

Sarah was immediately caught within the senses-inflaming web of sensuality Jake's kiss, his touch, wove about her. Curling her arms around his hips, she rolled onto her back, bringing him with her, into position between her parted thighs.

"You set me on fire, honey," Jake murmured as he lifted his mouth a hairbreadth from hers. "I have never, ever, become so hot, so hard, so fast."

Sarah made a soft sound, deep in her throat, and gently sank her teeth into his lower lip. "And I," she whispered, pausing to lave the spot with her tongue, "I have never, ever become so hot before . . . at all."

"Not even with your professor?" Jake asked, drawing his head back to gaze intently into her surprise-opened eyes.

Sarah blinked and shook her head. "No," she admitted, sinking her teeth into her own lower lip. "I, ah . . . you see, well, while I enjoyed being caressed and stroked, I . . ." She ran her tongue over her dry lips, then blurted out, "I never, ever had a . . . Ah, I never reached . . ." Her voice failed.

"You're kidding." Jake stared at her in astonishment. "Last night was your first—"

"Yes," Sarah interjected, feeling her cheeks growing warm. "My very first . . . with you."

"Hot damn!" Jake whooped, dipping his head to reward her with a quick, hard kiss. "And?" he demanded, raising his head to monitor her expression and her response.

"And?" Sarah frowned, uncomprehending.

Jake gave her a look of sheer disbelief. "And, what did you think, feel? Did you enjoy it?"

"*Enjoy* hardly describes it," Sarah answered, exhaling a deep sigh of satisfaction. "It was . . ." She hesitated, searching for a definitive word. "Everything." She smiled dreamily. "Everything I had always heard it was, but didn't believe could ever really be possible."

"Oh, Sarah." Jake's tone was humble. His eyes were soft, and his kiss was a benediction. But his body betrayed the solemn moment by leaping with renewed life. Jake raised his head to look at her with eyes now glittering with devilish intent. "Wanna experience that *everything* again?"

"Would Dan...Quayle?" she asked, innocently.

"Sarah," he said in a smiling warning.

"Does Tom...Cruise?"

"Sarah." Jake's smile gave way to laughter.

"Can Gregory...Peck?"

"That does it." Growling his appreciation, Jake pounced on her mouth and on her willing, eager body.

This time their lovemaking was hot and fast, hard and deep, wild and erotic, infinitely, thrillingly satisfying, and mentally and physically exhausting.

Entwined, locked together in the most intimate of embraces, their bodies spent in ultimate depletion, Sarah and Jake caressed and stroked each other to sleep.

Jake woke to bright sunshine and the muzzy realization that it had to be near, if not already past, noon.

He had to go to work!

The startling thought banished the last clinging wisps of sleep, and brought another, even more jolting realization of where he was. And where Jake was, exactly, was buried deep within the moist, encasing warmth of Sarah.

His body stirred, beginning to expand to fill her alluring sheath. Again? Jake blinked and grinned, both amazed and amused by the virile prowess he hadn't been aware of possessing. He wanted, longed, ached to test that heretofore unknown ability, but time decreed he postpone his test until another day, unless, unless...

Jake shot a hopeful glance at the small clock on the nightstand and sighed in disappointment. He had no time to spare wallowing in bed...and in Sarah. Heaving another sigh, he slowly eased himself from her, careful not to awaken her. A soft, loving expression crept over his face.

Sarah looked so peaceful, so vulnerable, in her slumber. Peaceful, vulnerable and... A streak of male pride lit a gleam in his eyes. Sarah looked so relaxed, so replete, so utterly, beautifully satisfied.

Lord, he hated to leave her. But leave her he must, he told himself. Sliding from the bed, he padded barefoot into the bathroom. After taking care of that business, he returned as silently to the bedroom to gather his clothes from the floor and get dressed.

Sarah woke, tossing the coverlet aside, stretching and yawning and testing the limits of his endurance and resolve. Catching sight of him, frozen in the act of shoving his arm into the sleeve of his jacket, she sat bolt upright. Frowning, she raked her fingers through her wildly tangled hair and asked, ''Where are you going?''

Out of my head if you don't cover your tempting self, Jake thought in silent despair. ''I have to go to work,'' he said, shrugging into the jacket.

"It's Sunday," Sarah protested. Then her frown darkened in consternation. "Isn't it?"

"Yes," Jake replied, in a voice strained by his inner battle to withdraw his avid gaze from the tantalizing allure of her luscious, naked body, her moist, parted, pouting lips. "But I still have to work."

"Oh." Sarah's lips turned down in a disappointed curve. "But you only had one day off."

Jake lost the inner battle, and made a visual feast of her. "I know." He smiled, inordinately pleased by the disappointment she wasn't even trying to conceal. "It's the way our schedule works. I get two days next week. Sunday and Monday."

She glanced at the clock. "What time do you start?"

"Three." Jake dragged his eyes from her form to the clock. The hands stood at 12:52. "I go off duty at midnight." He shifted his gaze back to her...face, and arched one eyebrow questioningly. "Will you miss me?"

Sarah tossed him a droll look. "Would a fish miss wa—?"

He cut her off, shaking his head and grinning. "Not again. Answer me, damn it. Will you miss me?"

Her fantastic eyes took on that pansy-velvet softness. "Yes, Jake." Her voice was just as soft. "I'll miss you." She shrugged. "But I have plenty of work to keep my mind occupied. I've got a pile of assigned essays on the Zhou dynasty to read and grade." Her lips took on the downward curve that so tugged at his heart. "Still, I'll miss you like hell."

His throat suddenly tight, Jake took a step toward her, then backed up again. Damn, he didn't want to go, he railed, adoring her with his eyes. "Er..." He cleared his throat. "What time do you take lunch tomorrow?"

Sarah gave him a distracted look.

"Was the question too difficult?" He clenched his hands into fists in an effort to keep himself from crossing the room to her.

"Cute," she muttered. "I get a break between classes at one on Mondays."

"Will you meet me at Dave's place for lunch?" he asked, keeping his eyes fastened on her face while edging back, toward the door.

"Will you kiss me goodbye?"

"I'm afraid to."

"Afraid!" Sarah cried. "Why?"

Jake snorted in a rueful, derisive way. "I'm afraid that if I kiss you, I'll never get out of here."

Sarah actually appeared to glow from his compliment. A mischievous smile tilted her lips. "Okay." She drove him wild by heaving her chest and breasts in a sigh. "Sorry, but, no kiss, no lunch."

"Sarah," Jake groaned, struggling to control a smile. "You're a hard woman."

"So I've been told," she retorted. "Now get your rump over here and give me a kiss."

"Man, oh, man," he groused. "The things a guy has to do to get a lousy lunch date." His dancing eyes belying the complaint, grateful for the excuse to do what he desperately wanted to do, Jake crossed to the bed, slid his arms under hers and hauled her up, crushing her breasts against his chest.

"Yes," Sarah said, raising her mouth for his kiss. "But remember what *I* had to do for a lousy dinner."

"You are definitely asking for it, honey," Jake said in warning, again losing the battle against laughter.

Her expression brightened with delighted surprise. "Yes, I am, aren't I? How wonderfully...freeing!"

Loving her like mad in that instant, sharing her delight, Jake took her mouth in a soul-enslaving, emotion-sealing, hair-curling kiss.

His body reacted to the kiss, the tentative touch of her tongue, in a normal, healthy, painful way, sending warning signals from his groin to his mind.

He *had* to get out of there.

Hearing the sharp inner command, Jake released her and beat a hasty retreat to the door.

"Tomorrow. Lunch. Be there," he panted.

Sarah had the nerve to taunt him. "Or?"

"Or I'll come looking for you," he threatened, yanking open the door and striding out of the room.

The exciting sound of Sarah's throaty laughter brought him up short, two strides beyond the doorway. Acting on sheer impulse, he spun and strode back to the doorway.

Sarah's eyes lit up at the sight of him, their revealing sparkle showing her approval of his impulse. "Jake?" She gave a tentative smile. "You look so odd, disturbed. Is... is something wrong?"

"No, honey." Jake shook his head and gulped a courage-gathering breath. "It's... er, I just thought you should know that..." He paused, then plunged ahead. "I love you. I love you like hell."

"Oh, Jake!" Sarah cried, moving to scramble from the bed. "I love you, too."

Go. Now. Or you'll never go.

"Tomorrow, love," Jake said, obeying the inner voice of reason by spinning away and literally running for the entrance door to the apartment.

The plaintive sound of Sarah's voice calling to him followed Jake from the apartment and down the stairs and echoed in his head inside the car. Motionless, he waited for the expected sinking reaction to his impetuous admission; it didn't materialize. What he felt was an expanding joy inside him in response to Sarah's reciprocal confession.

How could he leave her? Jake railed, staring sightlessly through the windshield. How could he force himself to go, now, after hearing her say she loved him? He ached to hold her, caress her, laugh with her, love her, make love to her, with her, all day, all night, forever.

His hand grasped the door handle; sheer willpower kept him from releasing the catch. Jake had to leave Sarah, and he knew it. He had a job, responsibilities, that he could not in good conscience simply ignore. And yet, missing her already, and greatly tempted to chuck the job, if only for the day, Jake gave a sharp shake of his head in self-denial. Then he fired the engine and switched on the citizens band radio, which was always set to the police frequency.

He'd call her during his dinner break, he promised himself, using the treat as a means to get himself in gear. The car moved forward into the deserted Sunday street. Jake handled the car smoothly but automatically.

His thoughts entangled with memories of the night and morning spent with Sarah, and the multifaceted, supremely satisfying results derived from it, Jake paid scant notice to the crackle issuing from the CB, until the voice of the day patrol officer sputtered from it, snaring his full attention.

Officer Jorge Luis was reporting in on his initial response to yet another car-stripping investigation.

Another? Jake shot a frowning glance at the CB just as Jorge reported the modus operandi of the theft. From what Jorge was saying, it was apparent that it was the second such crime he had investigated since Friday.

The second? Jake wondered when the other theft had occurred. Hell, he'd only been off one day—but somebody had been busy.

The MO was exactly the same as that of the theft Jake had investigated two days ago. Both cars, late-model luxury sedans, had been stripped down to the bare bones.

Amateurs. Jake again defined the thieves, an uneasy feeling curling in his gut. Damned if it wasn't shaping up as if they might be dealing with a local ring here.

Jake heaved a sigh and applied the brakes as he approached the red light at the intersection near his apartment. That was all they needed, he thought, tapping his fingertips on the steering wheel. A blasted ring of amateur parts thieves, looking to become professionals.

The light flicked from red to amber to green, and within that tiny pause, Jake got a hunch, and acted on it. Instead of turning right, onto the street where his apartment was located, he drove straight ahead, heading out of town.

Jake's destination was a junkyard situated on the fringe of the Sprucewood town limits, but within the town's police jurisdiction.

Maybe his hunch would prove groundless, Jake reflected. But, then again, it couldn't hurt to have a look-see, he figured, since doubt about the place already existed.

Not only Jake, but every other member of the department, had at one time or another expressed suspicions about the junkyard, and the irascible old coot who owned and operated it. The prevailing theory being that the place was used at times as an intermediary drop-off for stolen cars and parts ultimately headed for a chop shop in one of the larger nearby cities, like Norristown, Wilmington, Camden or—most likely—Philadelphia.

Acting on their suspicions, every member of the force, the chief included, had made a point of visiting the establishment off and on, and had come away empty. So, for that matter, had various officers of the state police.

But, what the hey, Jake mused, it still couldn't hurt to have a look around. Coming to another highway intersection, he made the turn onto an old, less traveled route that went right by the eyesore.

Jake slowed the car's speed as he approached the junkyard and began rubbernecking, checking out the fenced area, which was littered with mangled, rusting old heaps and spare parts. Nothing appeared unusual. In fact, it was as quiet as a church—an abandoned church. But then, he reminded himself, it was Sunday.

The car was barely moving, just creeping along, by the time he drove past the entrance to the yard. Risking a longer, more intensive look, Jake noticed three young men giving the once-over to the banged-up heaps parked at the very front of the junkyard, all of which had For Sale stickers plastered on their mostly cracked windshields.

Kids, Jake decided, probably from the college, looking for a jalopy with which to haunt the streets and hunt the girls. A smile twitched the corners of his mouth. Jake liked kids, all kids. Although, even from a distance, Jake could see that these were not really kids, but young men, likely college seniors, in their early twenties. It didn't matter. To Jake, as long as they were in school, from prekindergarten through college graduation, they were kids.

Wishing the trio luck in their hunt—for a car and for the girls—Jake eased his foot down on the accelerator, increasing the car's speed. A short distance farther along the highway, he pulled onto the lot of a deserted gas station, made a turn and drove off again, heading back to town.

Telling himself to get a move on or he'd be late for work, Jake slanted a cursory glance at the junkyard on his way by, and eased his foot off the gas pedal.

Now that's odd, he thought, frowning. The three young men he had noticed before were climbing into a gleaming new—and wildly expensive—black-and-silver van, customized with all the luxury extras, like miniblinds and curtains at the windows.

Both puzzled and curious, Jake took a hard, quick but comprehensive look at the man preparing to get into the driver's side of the sleek vehicle. From habit, he stored the man's vital statistics in his memory file: above medium height, slender, slightly muscular build, good-looking, long nose, strong jawline, dark hair and eyebrows, fading summer tan, no visible scars or identifying marks.

Got it. Now get moving, Jake advised himself, catching sight of the time on the dashboard clock. It was past one-thirty. He still had to shower, shave, get into uniform and... Jake's stomach emitted a low growl. He had better rustle up something to eat. It was time to get kicking.

Jake indulged himself reminiscing about Sarah during the drive back into town; he really had no choice, for she filled his mind to the exclusion of any other concerns.

It was incredible, he marveled, counting the number of days since he had first spotted her sitting in that corner booth at Dave's place, looking so studious and owlish, and so very appealing, in those oversize glasses.

Four days. Jake shook his head in wonder. Who'd have thought it? He grinned as he made the turn onto the street. Incredible? Ha! He laughed aloud. It was more like pretty damned amazing.

Who'd have thought it, indeed? he wondered, taking the steps to his apartment two at a time. Jake Wolfe, footloose and fancy-free, taking the leap from heart-whole to crazy in love in one giant bound.

Sarah. Lord, he did love her, Jake thought, tearing his clothes off as he strode from his front door to the bedroom.

Love at first sight? Well, perhaps not at *first* sight, Jake hedged, heading for the bathroom. Maybe not even at first dinner together. The second dinner, here at his place? Jake pondered the possibility as he adjusted the water temperature before stepping under the shower.

A vision filled his mind, sharp and clear, of those heated moments he'd had with her on the sofa after dinner Friday night. She had responded so sweetly, before breaking free to escape into the kitchen.

Yeah, he decided. It had probably begun on Friday.

Either way, his mother was going to be very smug about being proved correct, once she knew. Jake grimaced as he lathered shampoo into his hair. And his brothers... He groaned. His brothers were going to have a field day with it—and with him. Their baby brother, snared in love's trap, so to speak.

Oh, well... Jake shrugged and rinsed the mound of spring-rain-scented lather from his head. They'd change their tune in a hurry after they met Sarah.

Sarah.

The vision in his mind shifted to the night and the morning he had spent with her. Sarah was so...so magnificent in surrender, giving of herself with every living particle of her mind and body.

The steaming water pulsating from the shower jets cascaded down the length of Jake's body, triggering memories and images and sensations. The sluicing water revitalized his flesh. The feel of it recalled to his mind the silky feel of Sarah's satiny legs, sliding along his thighs, tautening his muscles, causing a quiver in the lightly sprinkled short hairs.

Lost in a dream of her, of the exquisite moments in her encircling embrace, his body joined with hers, his heart pounding, his pulse racing, Jake closed his eyes and reexperienced the wonder that was Sarah.

Love her? Jake drew a shuddering breath. No, he didn't love Sarah; he adored her.

His body responded predictably to his memories. He wanted her, here, now, with him, a part of him. Hurting from the intensity of his need for her, Jake arched his body and threw back his head. The pulsating water beat against his flesh, and poured into his open mouth, effectively swamping the memory flow.

"Damn fool!" Choking, coughing and laughing at himself, Jake turned off the water and stepped, dripping wet, onto the bath mat.

Boy, you've got a real case, he told himself, rubbing the water from his body with a large towel. You are definitely down for the count.

Shrugging, Jake tossed the towel in the direction of the hamper and sauntered into the bedroom. It didn't matter. Nothing mattered except Sarah.

Sarah.

A thought, a startling consideration, made Jake pause, his hand thrust inside his underwear drawer. Recalling her remark of earlier that morning about feeling wonderfully free, Jake mused that maybe, just maybe, you had to be willing to surrender your freedom to achieve the real meaning of being free.

Frowning over the concept, Jake glanced around the room, as if seeking truth. What he found was the face of the clock, just as the hands positioned themselves at 2:15.

Lord! He had no time to indulge in philosophical meanderings. He had to go to work!

Nine

***

She was in love.

Sarah spent the majority of the afternoon in a euphoric haze, marveling over the wonder of it all.

How was it possible? How had it happened? The questions arose to confront her; Sarah sidestepped them by telling herself that, even though she had never believed in the concept of love at first sight, it had happened, therefore it was possible.

End of questions. Besides, she felt too good, too well loved and satisfied to tax her brain and her emotions. In her estimation, Jake Wolfe epitomized everything that mattered to her. His senses-stirring attractiveness aside, Jake was kind, gentle, strong, honest, a joy to be with, to laugh with, and a veritable powerhouse of a lover.

The thought was arousing, and sent delicious shivers skipping up Sarah's spine and down her legs. Not again! Laughing silently at herself and the weakness the mere consideration of Jake could instill inside her, Sarah polished off a lunch of scrambled eggs and toast while telling herself to get busy.

Sarah had yet to as much as glance at the pile of essays waiting for her attention.

After Jake's precipitate flight, she had dawdled for nearly an hour, luxuriating in a tub filled to the rim with hot water and topped by a mound of perfumed bubbles. The heated water had soothed the tight achiness in her thigh muscles and the tenderness at their apex.

Jake was one masterful lover, Sarah had reflected, closing her eyes, floating in the tub of sensual recall. Beneath the waterline, the tips of her breasts had hardened into tight buds of pleasure aroused by the thrilling memories performing an erotic dance in her mind.

Sarah's sensitized flesh remembered the feel of Jake's hands, exploring every inch of her quivering body, his mouth, suckling greedily before moving on, seeking to know her, all of her, her deepest secrets.

The perfumed scent of the bath salts wafted on the steam, filling her senses. Sighing, Sarah moved slowly, sinuously, unconsciously reveling in the flow of silky water caressing her skin. Her thighs parted, her breathing grew shallow, quickening with the images playing inside her head, images of Jake, stroking her, loving her, possessing her, with his hot kisses, his thrusting tongue, his hard, powerful body.

A moan, low, needful, whispered through Sarah's parted tingling lips. The whimpering sound scattered the images, bringing her to her senses.

Memory melt. The realization of the hot moisture gathering in the depths of her femininity brought a self-conscious flush to Sarah's cheeks. She was ready for him, wanting him so much, she was shocking herself. Slamming her thighs together, she jolted upright, her movement so abrupt that she set the water lapping, splashing out over the rim of the tub.

Enough of the fantasizing, Sarah told herself, proceeding with her bath, and the subsequent mopping of the floor, with brisk, no-nonsense efficiency.

After her bath, she spent another half hour shampooing, conditioning and blow-drying her hair.

Then, her body not only replete, but clean and glowing with health and well-being, Sarah trailed into the kitchen to start a pot of coffee. While the aromatic brew dripped into the pot, she stared into space, a soft smile curving her lips, drifting in a dream of Jake.

Her first cup of coffee did revitalize Sarah somewhat, enough for her to wander to the front door and collect the Sunday paper from the hallway. But, although she carried the paper to the table by the window in the tiny dining area, she didn't so much as glance at the headlines. Secure and protected within a cocoon of exciting love, Sarah had no interest whatever in the machinations of the outside world.

Hugging her happiness close, she mooned about the apartment, absently touching things, plumping throw pillows, gazing out the window at the sparkling autumn afternoon until hunger drew her out of herself and into the kitchen.

Her meager meal consumed, Sarah carried her dishes to the sink, refilled her coffee cup and, picking up the paper as she passed the table, settled herself on the couch in the living room. The very first article to catch her eye burst her euphoric bubble of well-being and happiness.

The article gave an account of another car-stripping, which had occurred sometime Saturday night—last night, while she and Jake had been together.

Andrew.

The young man's name and image filled Sarah's mind and chilled her soul. Had Andrew and his two friends—? Her thought splintered as she shook her head.

It didn't make sense. Neither Andrew nor the other two men had any conceivable reason for stealing anything—let alone car parts, for goodness' sake.

And yet, and yet... Sarah shuddered at the memory of Andrew's threatening tone of voice, the expression of menace that had tightened his visage.

She knew, she just knew, there was a connection between the theft of the parts and the furtive look about the three friends, and Andrew's subsequent warning to her to be silent.

Jake.

Shoving the paper aside, Sarah jumped up to pace the length and width of the room, distractedly raking her hands through her neatly brushed hair.

She had agreed to meet Jake for lunch tomorrow but... Sarah bit her lip. Dave's place was so close to the campus, too close. Suppose Andrew were to see her with Jake? He might even recognize Jake as the police officer who patrolled the perimeters of the college grounds.

Sarah came to a dead stop, her mind shrieking a warning. She would have to contact Jake, tell him she couldn't meet him. She could not take the risk of placing him in danger.

He's a cop. The risk of danger is part of his job.

The inner voice of reason broke through the paralyzing mist of panic seeping into Sarah's mind, calming her frantic fears. Drawing a deep breath, she examined the inner assurance from a rational perspective.

Jake was a law-enforcement officer, a professional, trained and prepared to deal with criminals of all kinds. She herself had considered his qualities, his strengths, and decided that Jake was definitely hero material. What he and his brother officers did for a living might be scary for the women who loved them, but that was their problem... her problem....

Jake was tough and self-confident, supremely capable of taking care of himself, Sarah told herself sternly. And, instead of hanging back, avoiding him, she should risk the possibility of him ridiculing her intuition about the three men and tell Jake about her suspicions.

Really, Sarah chided herself, heaving a sigh of relief—what could Andrew do to her, anyway?

Her decision made, she left the papers scattered on the couch, collected her briefcase and returned to the table in the small corner near the window. She had work to do, and the day wasn't getting any younger.

Sarah had read and graded over half of the assigned essays, and was feeling pleased about the quality of most of them, when the phone rang, a little after seven.

Jake? Bright expectation sent her flying from her chair to the phone on the kitchen wall.

"Hello?" Her voice held a breathless, hopeful note.

"Hi." Jake's voice was low, sexy, hinting at remembered intimacy. "I couldn't wait until tomorrow," he murmured, robbing her of the little breath she possessed. "I had to at least talk to you before then."

"I...I'm glad," Sarah admitted, way beyond ingenuousness and game-playing.

"How are you?"

"Missing you."

Jake drew a sharp, audible breath. "I'm hurting," he confessed, exhaling a derisive chuckle. "Hell of a state for a man who's supposed to be working."

Sarah had a sudden, clear image of Jake as he had appeared earlier that morning, naked and gloriously aroused, and knew the state he was referring to. "Ah...where are you calling from?" she asked, in the hope of diverting the distracting, sensuous trend of her thoughts.

"The diner out on the highway. I'm on my supper break," he replied, in a more normal, less enticing tone. "Are you getting anywhere with your work?"

"I'm over halfway through the essays," she answered on a sigh of gratitude. "For the most part, they are really well written and quite good."

"The students must have a good teacher," Jake asserted, offering her a blatantly biased compliment.

Not nearly as good as the teacher the *teacher* had, Sarah reflected with arousing recall, while voicing a murmured "Thank you, I do my best."

"If memory serves," Jake drawled, "your best far surpasses excellence."

Sarah grew warm all over, warm and mush-minded. Her fingers plucked at the worn, soft jeans encasing her legs, and her misty-eyed gaze strayed, around the kitchen and through the archway, to collide with the papers strewn on the couch. The sight jolted her back to reality.

"Jake, stop," she protested, tearing her riveted stare from the papers.

"Stop what?" he asked with feigned innocence.

"You know what."

His soft laughter held the allure of forbidden delights. "Okay," he agreed. "What do you want to talk about?"

"Well..." Sarah hesitated, and an inner voice shouted, *Tell him. Now.* "Er... I read in the paper about the reports of two cars being stripped. Are you working on those?"

"Not at the moment," Jake's voice was dry as a rainless August, indicating his belief that she was merely trying to change the subject. "Why?"

"Well, I mean, two car-strippings in as many days..." she said, slowly leading up to the moment of disclosure.

"Three," he inserted.

"What?" Sarah blinked.

"There was another this morning," Jake explained. "I heard the day officer call in his report over my car CB on my way home from your place."

A glimmer of hope sprang into Sarah's mind. Maybe her intuition about the students was wrong. Maybe... Another consideration, this one for Jake's safety, sent a chill down her spine. She had to know, had to ask. "Do you believe you are dealing with professional thieves here?"

"Possibly." Jake sounded coolly unperturbed, almost nonchalant. "But I seriously doubt it."

"Why?" Sarah asked, feeling juxtaposed between the conflicting emotions of relief and renewed fear.

Jake chuckled tolerantly at her persistence. "Because all three of the thefts had all the earmarks of having been committed by rank amateurs."

Sarah frowned. "How would you know that?"

"Honey, they stripped the damn things," he answered patiently. "Real professionals would simply have swiped the entire car."

"Really?" Sarah was intrigued. "Why?"

"Easier," Jake replied, laughing softly. "Mere seconds are required for a professional to steal a car, locked or not. It can take minutes—a few or a lot, depending on the adeptness of the thief, or thieves—to strip a car down."

"Oh" was all Sarah could think of to say, because her mind was busy repeating the word *amateurs*. Her intuition had been correct—she now felt positive about it. She drew a long breath, preparing to lay her concerns on Jake's broad shoulders, but she didn't get a word out of her mouth.

"Oh, honey, I've got to hang up," Jake said. "The waitress just set my dinner on the counter."

"Oh...okay," Sarah said, feeling and sounding deflated.

Jake obviously attributed her tone to disappointment over having to disconnect, for he murmured, "I'll see you tomorrow at Dave's place."

"Yes." Resolve now colored her tone; she would definitely talk to him tomorrow.

"Good night, honey." Jake's voice indicated his reluctance to hang up.

"Good night," Sarah said on a sigh, sharing his reluctance. "You'd better go. Your meal will get cold."

"Not as cold as I feel at this moment." Jake's voice went low, intimate. "I need you to hold me, make love with me, warm me up, set me on fire."

"Oh, Jake," she whispered on a sigh.

"Oh, hell," he growled in return. "Good night, love."

Sarah heard a soft click, and then a dial tone. She closed her eyes, fumbled the receiver onto the cradle and sighed again. "Good night, love."

Nearly two hours later, Sarah's resolve was in shreds, and her fear was renewed and running rampant. She had just finished reading Andrew's essay. In and of itself, as a completed assignment, the essay was not merely good, it was brilliant—comprehensive, well written, and deserving of an A+. It was the central theme of the work that terrified Sarah.

Andrew's theme was power. Personal power. With the skill of a master weaver, he had woven that theme through the essay. The finished product could be likened to a written tapestry depicting the machinations of the feudal nobles who, by cleverly using their own power, had so weakened the power of the Zhou dynasty that China had declined into a confused mass of separate and contentious states.

In any other situation, with any other student, Sarah would have happily praised Andrew's accomplishment. But, having read between the lines, as well as the actual typewritten words, Sarah had garnered insight into Andrew's character. It was not a pretty or a reassuring sight.

To Sarah's mind, the picture of Andrew that emerged was that of a bright, confident, emotionally cold young man, playing mind games by testing his intelligence and sharpening his wits against the grindstone power of the status quo.

The last hopeful vestiges of lingering doubt in Sarah's mind were swept away by one reading of Andrew's essay. She also knew without a doubt that he was the driving force of the three students, directing and controlling the activities.

Sarah had repeatedly questioned her own intuition, her instincts, simply because there appeared to be no obvious reason for the men to engage in unlawful pursuits. Now she knew better. Andrew wasn't in it for the money, she theorized. In a strange way, he was gambling, betting he could outthink and outwit the authorities.

Sarah's theory scared the hell out of her. But she no longer gave thought to the possible danger to herself. Her primary concern was for Jake.

She could not tell him.

After gingerly stuffing Andrew's essay into her briefcase, as if afraid it might attack if she didn't get it safely contained, Sarah sat, staring and immobile, while her mind proceeded to summon up, with perfect recall, her phone conversation with Jake.

Rank amateurs, he had called the thieves. But it wasn't Jake's phrasing that had made an impression on her, it was his tone of voice. He had sounded so unconcerned, almost casual in his attitude toward the amateurs.

And Sarah felt a sinking certainty that there wasn't a thing casual about Andrew.

Sarah drew a shuddering breath and conjured up the worst possible scenario. What if she told Jake of her suspicions about Andrew, and his veiled threat, and, instead of laughing, he gave some credence to her fears? Or even just decided to humor her? Sarah knew the answer. Jake would commence an investigation, and with his casual attitude, and fully aware that the suspects were students, still young men, he would be at a disadvantage from the outset. Jake would be in the position of believing he was hunting a tabby cat, when in truth he'd be stalking a tiger. Jake might be hurt, even . . .

No. Sarah shook her head sharply back and forth, rejecting the scene. It would not happen, because she refused to allow it to happen.

She would obey Andrew's dictum and remain silent, Sarah decided, her course set. For, although she had likened him to a hero, Sarah had no intention of putting Jake to the test. Quite the opposite. She would do anything she had to do to protect him.

Sarah had spent a restless night, intermittently wakeful and half sleeping, tormented by nightmares. The same terrifying dream kept recurring, a dream in which she saw Jake sprawled on the floor in a dark place, wounded and bleeding. Yet no matter how hard she fought, strained, to get to him, something held her back, and she could not move.

Around five, jerking awake for the third time, her skin cold and clammy with perspiration, her pulse racing, the sound of her voice screaming Jake's name reverberating in her head, Sarah flung the twisted covers from her and dragged her depleted body from the bed.

While drinking an entire pot of coffee, Sarah finished reading and grading the last of the essays. After Andrew's, they were blessedly bland. Forgoing food, which she was certain would choke her, she bathed, dressed and left for school, the acrid aftertaste of too much coffee stinging the back of her throat, the effects of too little rest pricking her eyes.

Sarah spent the morning alternately racking her brain to remember her classroom subject matter, and shooting increasingly nervous glances at her watch. Inner conflict tore at her feeble composure. She longed to see Jake, to be with him, to crawl inside the haven of his strong embrace and hide there. And at the same time she was afraid to see him, afraid of inadvertently letting something slip, revealing her fears to him.

By the time her lunch break came, Sarah felt fragile, close to unraveling. The sight of Andrew's van, pulled up at a traffic light at the intersection near Dave's place, stopped her in her tracks as she approached the street, once again preparing to jaywalk across to the luncheonette. The added shock of seeing Jake on the opposite sidewalk, in uniform, propped against his patrol car, his hand raised to her in greeting, had the breathtaking effect of a hard blow to the heart.

Indecisive, wanting to turn tail and run, Sarah hesitated, teetering on the curb.

"Come on, honey," Jake called, motioning her forward with a wave. "Before the light changes."

Reluctant, yet feeling caught, without recourse, Sarah slowly crossed to him. From the corner of her eye, she saw the light change to green, the van creep forward. Her stomach clenching, she stepped onto the sidewalk.

"Hi." Jake's smile was soul-destroying.

Sarah opened her mouth to respond, then gasped in disbelief as, stepping to her, Jake swept her into his arms and kissed her, hard, full on her surprise-parted lips—just as the van slowly cruised past.

Jake's kiss was shattering to Sarah's already riddled nervous system. The fact that Andrew had been a witness to Jake's embrace and kiss compounded the shock.

Unwilling even to contemplate what Andrew thought, in what manner he might react, yet unable to think of little else, Sarah moved like an automaton when Jake steered her into the small restaurant.

"Have I outraged your sense of propriety?" Jake asked in a teasing whisper, urging her into the corner booth.

Grasping at the excuse he so innocently offered, Sarah swallowed, nodded, and stuttered in agreement. "I, er—I'm not used to being—ah, you know..."

"Affectionate in public?" Jake inserted, openly laughing at her stammering.

"Y-yes." Telling herself to get her head together, Sarah gulped for a calming breath.

"I'm sorry." Jake's hand, warm and comforting, covered hers. "But it seems like forever since I left you yesterday. I had to kiss you or explode."

"Oh, Jake." Wanting to bawl, Sarah forced her lips into a smile. "I missed you, too."

The laughter fled from his face and his eyes, replaced by an expression so intent, so loving, that it brought a rush of hot tears to Sarah's eyes and a wailing protest into her mind.

Damn Andrew and his stupid power games. Damn his threats. Damn him. Damn him.

"Hiya, folks, what are you going to have today?"

Dave's cheery greeting broke the chain of Sarah's angry, resentful thoughts. She looked up at him, then across the table at Jake. He grinned and handed the pasteboard menu to her. A frown knit her brow as she squinted, without her glasses, at the selections, which consisted mostly of sandwiches.

The very idea of food made Sarah's stomach roil. Still, knowing she had to make the effort, if only to stave off questions from Jake, she searched for the least digestion-offending item on the card.

"Sarah?"

"Ah . . ." Sarah swallowed the taste of bile. "I'm really not very hungry today." She managed a weak smile for Dave. "Do you have a soup of the day?"

"Yep." Dave nodded emphatically. "Split pea with ham. I made it myself this morning."

"I'll have that," she said, setting the menu aside.

"That's all?" Jake scowled. "A bowl of soup isn't enough to get you through the rest of the day."

"Yes, it is." Not looking at Jake, she smiled at Dave. "Just the soup, please. Oh, and a small glass of milk," she added, hoping to neutralize the coffee seemingly burning a hole in the floor of her stomach.

"Yes, ma'am." Dave smiled back at her before turning his attention to Jake. "What about you?"

"The usual."

Dave grinned. "Two Coney Island dogs and a chocolate shake. Right?"

"You got it."

Sarah suppressed a shudder, and the urge to comment on his less-than-nutritious choices.

"So, did you get through that pile of essays?" Jake asked the minute Dave turned away.

The essays. Andrew. Sarah was forced to suppress another, deeper shudder. "Yes," she replied, in that instant coming to a firm decision born of frustration and anger.

Andrew would have to be dealt with. And she, not Jake, was going to do the dealing.

"So?" Jake nudged at her wandering attention.

"So...what?" Sarah frowned and fingered her paper napkin, tearing it; her decision carried with it a boatload of anxiety-causing baggage.

"So...how were they?" Jake frowned and shifted his gaze from her picking fingers to her eyes.

Sarah shifted her gaze, fearful of betraying herself, her anxieties. "They were very good. I didn't give a grade under a B —."

"What's wrong, honey?"

Sarah felt her eyelashes flicker, and drew on every ounce of control she possessed to keep her voice even, natural. "Wrong? Nothing. Why?"

"You're acting strange, nervous." Jake frowned. "Almost as if I make you uneasy."

"You? That's ridiculous." She pulled off a strained laugh and a fairly reasonable shrug. "I didn't sleep too well, that's all. But other than that..." She let her voice trail away, and shrugged again. "I'm fine."

Although Jake's expression said clearly that he was unconvinced, to Sarah's heartfelt relief he didn't pursue the subject. But a strained tension lay between them all through the interminable meal. Through sheer application, Sarah managed to consume every drop of her soup and milk, and even one of the crackers from the packet Dave served with the soup. But she felt utterly exhausted when, at last, she slid another of many glances at her watch and saw with relief that it was time for her to return to the campus.

"I...er, I've got to go," she said, avoiding Jake's eyes as she collected her things. "I've got a class in less than half an hour."

"How about tomorrow, same time, same place?" Jake asked, tossing enough bills on the table to cover the check and a generous tip for Dave.

"I'm...not sure," Sarah hedged, scouring her mind for an excuse as she slid off the seat. "Ah, I seem to recall the department head saying something about a faculty meeting." She walked determinedly toward the door, talking to him over her shoulder. "Could I give you a call at home before I leave in the morning?"

"Sure." Both Jake's tone and his expression were strained. "Honey, hold up a minute," he said, reaching out to grasp her arm as she pushed through the doorway and started across the sidewalk.

"I've got to go, Jake." Sarah could hear the desperation in her voice. "I'll call you." Pulling away from his hand, she stepped into the street. She had taken four long steps when the loud sound of screeching tires drew her head around, and she saw the vehicle streak through the intersection.

Andrew's van was aimed directly at her!

"Sarah!"

Ten

─────

With the harsh sound of his shout ringing in his head, his heart racing in his chest and his throat closing around a lump of fear, Jake sprinted after Sarah.

It was over in seconds, yet it seemed to go on forever. Everything blurred, yet remained clearly defined within the depths of his subconscious.

Jake caught a flash of black and silver. The large vehicle was bearing down on Sarah. There was no time to think. Tasting stark and absolute terror for the first time in his life, Jake reacted. Dashing in front of her, he shoved Sarah back, out of harm's way, instantly taking a flying leap after her to gain his own safety.

The vehicle sped past, missing Jake by mere inches. A moment stretched into eternity. Sarah lay in a shuddering heap near his shoulder. Reactive tremors rippling through his body, he pushed himself to his knees, simultaneously reaching for Sarah with unsteady hands. Taking her with him, he stumbled, steadied himself, and stood up.

"Holy—"

"Jake, are you all right?" Sarah cried, running her hands over his shoulders and down his chest.

"Yeah, yeah, I'm okay," he assured her, clasping her head in his hands to peer into her face. "Are you hurt?"

"A scrape... My knee..." Sarah was gasping for breath. "Oh, Jake, I was so frightened. The way you were flung to the street... I thought he had struck you!"

Jake exhaled a shaky laugh. "I did the flinging. That driver must either be drunk or drugged out of his mind." He paused to grab a breath. "Did you happen to get a look at the licence number?"

"No," Sarah said tremulously. "Did you?"

"No." Jake heaved a sigh. "I didn't even get a make on the vehicle. It all happened too fast."

"Y—yes."

Sarah was white as a sheet, and her eyes were wide, owlish-looking—even without the big round glasses. Sliding his hands to her arms, Jake started toward the sidewalk. "Let's go back inside, honey. You need to sit down."

"No." Shaking her head, Sarah came to an abrupt halt. "I'm all right." She turned to face the street again.

"Sarah, wait." He held her still when she would have walked away.

"I can't." Her expression was set in adamant lines. "I'm okay, and I've got a class. I'll call you." Pulling her arm free, she scanned the street and hurried away.

Almost, Jake thought, staring after her, as if she were running away... from him.

But then, Sarah had appeared to be shying away from him since before, and during, lunch, Jake mused, watching her as she cut across the campus.

What in hell?

Rattled from the near miss by the careening vehicle, and confused by Sarah's odd behavior, Jake stood staring across the way for long seconds after Sarah disappeared from his sight. A strange something niggled at the edges of his consciousness, tapping, as if for his attention.

But at that moment all Jake's attention was centered on Sarah. What had happened within the last twenty-odd hours to so unnerve her? Because Sarah had been nervous. And the baffling part was, she had seemed to be nervous of him.

Jake shook his head, as though in the hope of clearing his mind. It didn't make sense. Not after the night and morning they had spent together, laughing, loving. And she had sounded fine, relaxed and affectionate, when he had talked to her on the phone last night.

But she had said she hadn't slept well, Jake recalled, feeling a sudden emptiness. Was Sarah suffering misgivings about their shared intimacy, their declaration of love for one another?

For a moment, a long moment, Jake felt physically sick. Then reason asserted itself, chasing the nausea. Sarah's reaction to that near miss had not been that of a woman having second thoughts about her lover.

But, if it wasn't their relationship, what was bugging Sarah? He knew that something sure as hell was.

The persistent niggling at the back of Jake's mind tapped harder, seeking recognition.

Jake frowned and shrugged the uneasy sensation aside. He didn't have time to probe the inner workings of his gray matter. His primary concern was for Sarah.

Heaving an impatient sigh, Jake raised his arm to massage the tension-taut muscles twanging at the back of his neck. His gaze glanced off, then returned to, the black material covering his arm.

The uniform. Jake's thoughts swirled back to the morning he had first noticed Sarah sitting in the back booth inside the very restaurant he was standing in front of at that moment. An image formed of her behavior that morning when Dave introduced them. Sarah had appeared unnerved by him then, too. Memory nudged, and Jake recalled that he had pondered the possibility of Sarah being uneasy because of his uniform.

Of course, Jake had dismissed the idea as ridiculous. Now he wasn't so sure. But why would the sight of a police uniform unsettle someone—unless that someone had something to fear from the law?

But what, by any stretch of the imagination, could Sarah have to fear from the law...and therefore from him?

Though, admittedly, Jake had known Sarah a very short time, he felt he knew her very well. And the Sarah he felt he knew had nothing to fear from the law, or from him—most especially from him.

Why then did she appear so nervous while in his company when he was in uniform?

Damn strange, Jake mused, sparing a glance at his watch. There was still some time before he began his shift. Hoping to be able to spend more time with Sarah, he had dressed for work early, and had even picked up his patrol car before coming to meet her. He had time to ponder the puzzle.

Frustration eating at him, the niggling at the edge of his consciousness continuing to tap away, Jake walked to the car, slid behind the wheel and then sat, still as a stone, staring straight ahead, into the middle distance.

Sarah.

It simply didn't make sense.

Jake had never been able to tolerate things that didn't make sense. And so, in any instance, situation, happenstance, that made no sense, he would mentally pick at it, poke it, turn it inside out until it did make sense.

Perhaps that was why he enjoyed being a cop, Jake theorized, unaware of the everyday movement of people and traffic around him. Plodding though it often was, he enjoyed the process of systematic elimination to attain resolution of any given problem.

Okay, Mr. Law Officer, do your enjoyable thing, Jake told himself. Eliminate. Take it apart. Then put it back together. The beginning might be a good place to start.

Sinking into a plodding mode, Jake mentally ticked off the particulars.

Sarah, nervous and visibly uneasy on being introduced to him Thursday morning. Sarah, relaxed and at ease with him when he invited himself to dinner Thursday evening. Sarah, hesitant and uncertain Friday morning about accepting his invitation to have dinner with him. Sarah, relaxed and at ease with him at his place Friday evening. Sarah, vague and unsure about going out with him Saturday evening. Sarah, relaxed and at ease with him Saturday evening—and positively abandoned with him later, both Saturday night and Sunday morning. Then Sarah this morning, once again nervous and uneasy with him.

Damn! It still didn't ma—

It was at that split second that the niggling poked a hole in the veil of Jake's subconscious. He had a fleeting image of a large vehicle, saw a flash of black and silver, heard the echo of Sarah's cry.

"I thought he had struck you!"

He? Jake repeated in silent contemplation. He hadn't given any thought to the term at the time; it would be natural for her, or anyone, to speak of the driver as *he*. But, just for the sake of supposition, could Sarah have been referring to one particular he—a he she knew and possibly feared?

Farfetched? Way out? Sure, Jake conceded. But, on the other hand, what if— Jake blinked, and realized he was staring intently at the intersection. His subconscious replayed the scene for his conscious mind.

He could hear again the screech of tires as the van shot forward, see the flash of black and silver, feel the stark terror gripping him. A reactive shiver streaked up his spine, causing the short hairs at the back of his neck to quiver.

That driver had been neither drunk nor drugged senseless. He had made a deliberate attempt to run Sarah down!

Van? Jake frowned. Now, where . . .

Black and silver!

Jake's subconscious replayed another hidden memory. He could see the black-and-silver van of yesterday morning, and the young men getting into it, young men he had immediately assumed were college kids.

And Sarah taught at the college.

Coincidence? Jake made a snorting noise. Coincidence be damned! Now it was beginning to make a little sense. But he needed to plod a little further, probe a little deeper.

On first spotting the kids—the young men—at the junkyard, Jake had thought they were looking for some cruising wheels. And so it had struck him as odd when, after turning around, he saw them piling into that expensive van. Why, he'd reflected, since they already had the use of that love boat on wheels, would they be looking at wrecks in a junkyard?

Jake made a face. Just another thing that didn't make— Jake jolted erect in the seat. The junkyard! The very same junkyard that every local police officer suspected was being used to fence stolen cars and parts! Could it possibly be that those college kids were the amateurs committing the thefts?

Jake quivered, not unlike a bloodhound that has picked up the scent of a fugitive. His instincts screamed that he was on to something. But wait, he cautioned himself. Even if those three young men were the thieves, where did Sarah fit into the picture? he asked himself. Nothing, no one, would ever convince him that Sarah was involved in the crimes.

A blank wall. Jake sighed, then went still as another possibility worked its way to the forefront of his mind. What if Sarah had inadvertently seen or heard something . . . something indicating the men's involvement or intent?

It was all supposition, of course, but...damn, Jake thought, grimacing at a seeming error in his deductions. Sarah had shown agitation and nervousness around him on Thursday morning, and the first of the thefts had been reported on Friday. Well, that killed that theory, he thought dejectedly. Unless . . . unless there had been other, previous thefts, outside the jurisdiction of the Sprucewood police force.

He needed to talk to Sarah.

Cursing the necessity of waiting until his supper break, Jake fired the engine, checked for oncoming traffic, then pulled the car into the street. Waiting would not be easy, but in the meantime, he had a job to do.

Before he spoke to Sarah, Jake decided to check the wire for any reported thefts of car parts within a reasonable striking distance of Sprucewood.

It was late, close to twilight. Sarah's last class had ended hours ago, and still she sat in her small office, her insides and her hands shaking.

The tremors rippling through Sarah were no longer in direct relation to the terrifying incident of earlier that afternoon, although her brush with death had initiated the process. But as the day crept on, a subtle change had occurred within her, altering her fear, transforming it into anger.

Now, as evening approached, Sarah's anger had reached a level of sheer rage, rage at Andrew Hollings, the intelligent student who had out-smarted himself by attempting murder. And Sarah labored under no illusions concerning Andrew's motivations; he had coldly, deliberately tried to run her down.

Andrew's attempt on Sarah's life was damning enough in her eyes. But even more damning was the frightening realization that Andrew had come within inches of killing Jake—even if inadvertently.

Andrew's criminal and destructive activities had to be stopped, and Sarah had come to the conclusion that, since she was the only person aware of what he was up to, she was the only one who could stop him.

But first she needed proof, something concrete that she could present to the authorities, to Jake. It was her need for evidence, and a method of gathering it, that had kept Sarah sitting quietly in her darkening office ever since she had dismissed her last class for the day.

After examining, then rejecting, several ideas, Sarah settled on the one method she thought just might work. That method came to mind along with a memory of something Jake had said about one of his brothers being an undercover cop with the Philadelphia police.

Sarah reached for the phone on her desk and punched in the extension number for the college admissions office. Minutes later, she replaced the receiver, then jotted down Andrew Hollings's address on a notepad. A small, grim smile curling her lips, Sarah pushed out of her chair and strode from the office. She had to hurry home and get her car out of the garage; she had a job of surveillance to do.

Pay dirt—on two fronts. Satisfaction lightening his step, Jake loped from the police station and got back into his car. A check of the AP wire had given him information about two separate car-parts thefts, the first ten days ago in the nearby town of Valley View, the second in the Philadelphia bedroom community of Golf Acres, located some thirty miles west of Sprucewood.

Jake's second front had been the head of the Sprucewood College security force, who had provided Jake with the make, model and year of the black-and-silver van, in addition to the name and address of its owner.

Andrew Hollings. Jake rolled the name around in his head as he pulled the car into the lot at the diner. He had every intention of checking out the digs of one Mr. Andrew Hollings. But first, he needed to talk to Sarah.

It was dark, and cold, and kind of scary—too close to Halloween for comfort, Sarah reflected, even if she did appear dressed for the upcoming All Saints' Eve celebration, in boots, old jeans and a bomber jacket, a knit cap hugging her head, hiding her hair.

Perhaps she should have taken a few minutes to stop by the variety store to purchase a fright mask and gone the whole undercover route.

Laughing softly at the fanciful thought, Sarah drew her coat more closely around her shivering body and peered through the windshield at the large Victorian house that had been converted into student apartments.

Andrew shared one of those apartments with his two friends. The black-and-silver van was parked at the curb in front of the building.

Was she on a fool's errand? Sarah asked herself, ignoring the grumble of hunger from her stomach and settling more comfortably in the driver's seat of her small car. Suppose she sat there all night and none of the men ever left the apartment? What would she do then?

Probably starve to death, Sarah thought wryly, rubbing her palm over her empty middle.

Where in hell was she? Jake fumed, listening to the twelfth ring of Sarah's phone. After the fifteenth ring, he slammed out of the diner and stormed back to the patrol car. It was after seven, and Sarah hadn't mentioned anything about having plans for the evening. Where could she be?

With a friend. At a meeting. Shopping. Get a grip, Wolfe, Jake told himself, tamping down an expanding sense of incipient panic. Sarah could have had any number of things to do. She was an adult, and fully capable of taking care of herself. Just because he loved her, he berated himself, that didn't mean she had to clear her plans with him. They weren't attached at the hip, for Pete's sake.

He'd have to wait until tomorrow morning, when she called him. As a rule, Jake could endure waiting for just about anything. But, damn, he railed, he hated waiting to hear from Sarah, especially tonight. The imposed wait caused a crawly sensation in Jake's gut. He didn't like the feeling. Cursing softly, he headed the car in the direction of the address passed on to him by campus security. It was a slow night, and the CB was quiet—for the moment. Jake was on his supper break. Maybe he'd spend the time checking out the place where Hollings lived.

Sarah was sorely tempted to turn on the engine, run the car heater, if only long enough to warm her cold-stiffened fingers and toes. Keeping her riveted stare fixed on the front entrance to the apartment, she reached for the ignition key. She froze in place, fingers gripping the key, as Andrew and his friends came out of the building and strode along the walkway to the sidewalk and the van parked alongside it.

Her breathing shallow, uneven, Sarah watched as the three men got into the van. The headlights flared on, and then the vehicle began to move. Sarah hesitated a moment, two and then, her fingers trembling, she fired the engine and, careful to keep at a safe distance, followed the van.

Jake had no sooner brought the car to a stop near the intersection closest to the apartment building when three men came striding out, piled into the black-and-silver van and drove away.

Interesting, he mused, giving the van the once-over as it cruised through the intersection. Deciding to tag along for a spell, Jake reached for the ignition, then paused as a small car fell into line behind the van.

Damned interesting. Starting the engine, Jake eased the patrol car into the street and around the corner, bringing up the rear of the curious procession.

The van led the way out of town, onto a secondary road, into the countryside. After passing a field of drying cornstalks, the van turned onto a dirt track. It glided to a stop beside a tumble down barn. The other, smaller car drove right on by, Jake noted with some satisfaction.

Jake was familiar with the property, and the structure, which was really only half a barn, since the other half had been destroyed by fire a couple of years ago.

Now, what business would three young men have poking around a deserted, burned-out barn? Jake asked himself, feeling certain he knew the answer. Hell, half a barn was better than nothing, when you needed a place to stash some hot car parts temporarily—wasn't it?

Sighing at the audacity of the young, Jake brought the car to a stop on the dirt shoulder of the road, got on the CB, gave a low-voiced report, then stepped out of the car. Moving with silent swiftness, he approached the closed, upright side of the barn, his hand dropping to unsnap the flap over the butt of his police revolver—just in case.

Sarah twisted her head around to mark where the van had turned, but continued on her way for about a quarter of a mile. Making a tight U-turn on the narrow road, she drove back, bringing the car to a stop near the dirt track. Her heart pounding inside her breath-constricted chest, she left the car, dashed across the road and crept along the track. Stopping midway to scoop up a stout stick—should she need to stand and defend herself, Sarah thought, a bit hysterically—she then resumed her creeping pace to the barn.

Jake could hear the low mutter of male voices from the other side of the barn wall. A yellowish-gold beam from a flashlight skipped over the cracks in the weathered boards. Standing in the pitch-blackness near the gaping, burned-out end of the wall, he eased his revolver from the holster, then stepped around the sagging wall.

"Police," Jake called out in a commanding voice, skimming a glance over the area to place the men. Though he spotted the cluttered heap of car parts, his nerves tightened when he realized he could pinpoint only two of the men. But the tightness didn't reveal itself in his stern expression or his hard voice. "Don't move. Don't even think about it."

Jake? Sarah's steps faltered at the sound of his voice. How—? What—? Rushing forward, she came up to the barn on the other side of the standing wall. Peering around the edge of the charred plank, she saw Jake standing in the opening opposite, his pistol drawn and leveled on Andrew's two friends.

But where was Andrew?

Even as the question filled her mind, Sarah caught sight of him, a tire iron in his raised hand, inching along the shadowed inside of the wall . . . heading for Jake.

Stifling a shocked gasp, and without pausing to think of her own safety, Sarah lifted the stick above her head and ran into the barn, directly at Andrew.

"Hey!" one young man exclaimed.

"What the—?" the other shouted.

Andrew screamed as the thick stick sliced through the air and struck the tire iron from his hand.

"Sarah!" Jake's voice wore a heavy coating of fear. "Get the hell over here, behind me!" While keeping his eyes fastened on the men, he reached out, clasped her by the wrist and literally swung her around and behind him.

"Jake...I..." Sarah began, only to be silenced by the harsh sound of his voice.

"You, Hollings, stop whining and get your ass over there beside your buddies." Jake smiled; the three young men blanched. "Just give me an excuse," he said, sounding not at all like a nice man. "If one of you moves, or even breathes heavy, I'll drop all three of you. *Then* I'll read you your rights."

The three men suddenly appeared to be cast in cement. Fighting a nervous giggle, Sarah leaned forward, to whisper over Jake's shoulder.

"My hero."

"Bag it, honey," Jake retorted in a murmur.

Stepping around to stand beside him, Sarah shot a glare at Andrew, and then asked Jake, "Can you manage all three of them by yourself?"

Jake slid a glittery look at her.

"Well, can you?" she persisted.

"Is Joel ... Grey?"

At that precise instant, as if to punctuate Jake's dry-voiced query, the wail of a police car siren broke the silence of the autumn night.

"Lord, I'm hungry," Jake groused, draping an arm over Sarah's shoulders as he escorted her to her car.

It was over. Sarah felt as though she had been tumbled through a harvester, bundled and banded. And she still had to explain the whole thing to Jake and the authorities. Apart from that, though, she felt pretty good ... and hungry, too.

"And me," she said, tightening the arm she had slung around his waist. "I didn't have dinner."

"Me either." Jake sighed. "I decided to use my break time to do a bit of sleuthing."

"I'm glad you did." Sarah tilted her head to look at him. "I don't suppose Dave's is open at this time of night?"

"No, he closes at six," Jake said, coming to a halt next to the driver's side of her car. "But the diner's open."

"Can you take the time?"

"Well, sure," Jake said, grinning at her. "I'm entitled to a supper break."

"Good. I'll meet you there." Sarah pulled the door open and slid behind the wheel. "Last one there pays the check," she called, firing the engine as she shut the door.

"I'll get you for that," Jake shouted after her as she pulled away from him. "And you'll love every minute of it."

And Sarah most certainly did.

"I like your method of getting even." Sarah stretched with slow, deliberate sensuality, and smiled with revealing satisfaction and repletion.

Over forty-eight hours had elapsed since the night of Andrew's and his friends' apprehension . . . and Jake's teasing promise to *get* her for tricking him.

And get her he had, in every way his fertile imagination could conceive of, all of which had excited Sarah to an unbelievable degree.

It was Jake's day off, and they had spent the hours, and themselves, in his bed.

Now, nearing midnight, his body still buried deep within hers, Jake raised his head from the satiny pillow of her breasts and grinned at her . . . looking both sleepy and rakish.

"And I like your sweet surrender to my methods." Lowering his head, Jake brushed his lips over hers, then groaning, captured her mouth in a searing kiss.

With a sense of disbelief and wonder, Sarah felt Jake's body quicken with hard renewal deep inside her, inciting an instant response from her.

"Again?" She stared at him in astonishment.

"Wild, huh?" Jake's expression revealed his own sense of amazement. "But I just can't seem to get enough of you." His gaze intent, watching for her reaction, he moved his hips. A satisfied smile tilted his lips when she arched into his gentle thrust.

"I . . . I can't seem to get enough of you, either," Sarah admitted, grasping his tight buttocks to draw him fully into her aching hunger.

His muscles growing taut with increasing desire, Jake thrust to the very core of her femininity. "Do you think we're simply insatiable?" he asked, in a voice rendered harsh by his constricting breath. "Or do you think there could be another reason for this unending need for each other?''

''What other reason?'' Sarah asked, knowing the answer, but longing to hear it again.

''Love?'' Stilling, Jake stared into her passion-bright eyes. ''I do love you, Sarah. Not just your body, and the pleasure it gives me, but your heart, and your mind and everything else that makes up my Sarah.''

Tears filmed Sarah's eyes, blurring the image of his adored face. ''And I love you, Jake Wolfe, in every possible way there is to love a man. I want to be with you forever.''

Holding desire at bay, Jake sealed her fate with a gentle kiss of promise. When he raised his head, his own eyes were suspiciously bright, even though a grin tugged at his lips.

''I hope forever takes a long time in coming. Loving you, the waiting for it will be heaven.''

* * * * *

SILHOUETTE® *Desire*

MAN OF THE MONTH: 1993

**They're tough, they're sexy...
and they know how to get the
job done....
Caution: They're**

MEN AT WORK

Blue collar... white collar... these men are working overtime
to earn your love.

July:	Undercover agent Zeke Daniels in Annette Broadrick's ZEKE
August:	Aircraft executive Steven Ryker in Diana Palmer's NIGHT OF LOVE
September:	Entrepreneur Joshua Cameron in Ann Major's WILD HONEY
October:	Cowboy Jake Tallman in Cait London's THE SEDUCTION OF JAKE TALLMAN
November:	Rancher Tweed Brown in Lass Small's TWEED
December:	Engineer Mac McLachlan in BJ James's ANOTHER TIME, ANOTHER PLACE

Let these men make a direct deposit into your heart.
MEN AT WORK... only from Silhouette Desire!

SILHOUETTE® Desire™

ANN MAJOR
SOMETHING WILD

Take a walk on the *wild* side with Ann Major's sizzling stories featuring Honey, Midnight...and Innocence!

September 1993 WILD HONEY
Man of the Month
A clash of wills sets the stage for an electrifying romance for J. K. Cameron and Honey Wyatt.

November 1993 WILD MIDNIGHT
Heat Up Your Winter
A bittersweet reunion turns into a once-in-a-lifetime adventure for Lacy Douglas and Johnny Midnight.

February 1994 WILD INNOCENCE
Man of the Month
One man's return sets off a startling chain of events for Innocence Lescuer and Raven Wyatt.

Let your wilder side take over with this exciting series—only from Silhouette Desire!

Silhouette Books has done it again!

Opening night in October has never been as exciting! Come watch as the curtain rises and romance flourishes when the stars of tomorrow make their debuts today!

Revel in Jodi O'Donnell's STILL SWEET ON HIM—
Silhouette Romance #969
...as Callie Farrell's renovation of the family homestead leads her straight into the arms of teenage crush Drew Barnett!

Tingle with Carol Devine's BEAUTY AND THE BEASTMASTER—
Silhouette Desire #816
...as legal eagle Amanda Tarkington is carried off by wrestler Bram Masterson!

Thrill to Elyn Day's A BED OF ROSES—
Silhouette Special Edition #846
...as Dana Whitaker's body and soul are healed by sexy physical therapist Michael Gordon!

Believe when Kylie Brant's McLAIN'S LAW —
Silhouette Intimate Moments #528
...takes you into detective Connor McLain's life as he falls for psychic—and suspect—Michele Easton!

Catch the classics of tomorrow—*premiering* today—
only from ▼ Silhouette

TAKE A WALK ON THE
DARK SIDE OF LOVE WITH

October is the shivery season, when chill winds blow and shadows walk the night. Come along with us into a haunting world where love and danger go hand in hand, where passions will thrill you and dangers will chill you. Silhouette's second annual collection from the dark side of love brings you three perfectly haunting tales from three of our most bewitching authors:

Kathleen Korbel
Carla Cassidy
Lori Herter

Haunting a store near you this October.

Only from ▼*Silhouette*® where passion lives.